WITHOUT WARNING

Beneath the carriage cover, the light was dim. It was like being in a very small tent, and it was rather more intimate than Sarah thought was wise. There was nothing for it, however, but to wait a few minutes and see whether the storm would pass. They would get soaked to the skin if they removed the cover and attempted to drive.

She looked down at her damp skirts and grinned. "Even when I try to dress like a lady, I inevitably end up looking the hoyden, do I not?" she asked breathlessly, turning to face Lord William.

When she saw the look on his face, a follow-up quip died on her lips. He was observing her as though he had just crossed a desert and she was a large, cold pitcher of ale.

"You look nothing like a hoyden, Lady Sarah," he said, his voice a husky rasp. Then, without warning, he lowered his head to hers and kissed her.

BOOK YOUR PLACE ON OUR WEBSITE AND MAKE THE READING CONNECTION!

We've created a customized website just for our very special readers, where you can get the inside scoop on everything that's going on with Zebra, Pinnacle and Kensington books.

When you come online, you'll have the exciting opportunity to:

- View covers of upcoming books
- Read sample chapters
- Learn about our future publishing schedule (listed by publication month *and author*)
- Find out when your favorite authors will be visiting a city near you
- Search for and order backlist books from our online catalog
- Check out author bios and background information
- Send e-mail to your favorite authors
- Meet the Kensington staff online
- Join us in weekly chats with authors, readers and other guests
- Get writing guidelines
- AND MUCH MORE!

**Visit our website at
http://www.kensingtonbooks.com**

AN HONORABLE MATCH

LAURA PAQUET

ZEBRA BOOKS
KENSINGTON PUBLISHING CORP.
www.kensingtonbooks.com

ZEBRA BOOKS are published by

Kensington Publishing Corp.
850 Third Avenue
New York, NY 10022

All Kensington titles, imprints and distributed lines are available at special quantity discounts for bulk purchases for sales promotion, premiums, fund-raising, educational or institutional use.

Special book excerpts or customized printings can also be created to fit specific needs. For details, write or phone the office of the Kensington Special Sales Manager: Kensington Publishing Corp., 850 Third Avenue, New York, NY 10022. Attn. Special Sales Department. Phone: 1-800-221-2647.

Zebra and the Z logo Reg. U.S. Pat. & TM Off.

First Printing: September 2004
10 9 8 7 6 5 4 3 2 1

Printed in the United States of America

ONE

The water crashed against the side of the ship, and the whole vessel heaved to the side. William usually didn't mind traveling the Mediterranean, but this voyage seemed particularly rough. Thank heaven he had never had occasion to cross the Atlantic.

An odd knocking began somewhere above his head, as though a lamp or some other fixture had come loose and was smashing against the hull of the ship. Lord knew, that could be possible, given the way the vessel was pitching about, but there was something odd about this knocking. It seemed faint but persistent, and it didn't occur in the same rhythm as the rest of the ship's noises.

It grew louder.

William twisted in his hard bunk. At least he didn't have to sleep in a rope hammock, like the crew, but there were times when he wondered whether such a sling would be more comfortable than a rock-hard mattress bolted to a frame that was bolted to the floor.

The knocking suddenly stopped. In its place, he heard the roar of a human voice.

"William!"

What on earth was George doing on this ship? George had no business to conduct in Athens.

Suddenly, William shot upright in bed. The ship he'd been dreaming of dissolved, replaced by the darkness of his bedroom in London. He touched the guttered candle next to his bed and found it cool. It had long since gone out, meaning it was very, very late.

Not again.

"Wills!" George's voice echoed in the small foyer, where Stinson was no doubt doing his best to dissuade George from entering. One might as well try to stop the sun from rising as prevent the Duke of Cambermere from doing something he'd taken it into his mind to accomplish.

"For God's sake, man, stop hushing me and fetch my brother."

William sighed and threw back the heavy coverlet. It was a shame, really, that George never took it into his mind to accomplish anything *useful.*

"It's all right, Stinson," he called out. "I'm awake."

Stinson, who served as both butler and valet in William's compact bachelor's chambers, appeared almost immediately in the doorframe. His face was stony. "I tried, my lord, but—"

Shoving his feet over the edge of the bed, William reached for the silk banyan Stinson held out to him. "Don't worry," he reassured the servant as an infinite weariness settled over him. "George is in full bore. There's nothing you could have done, short of shooting him."

"Is that any way to talk about your favorite brother?" George poked his head around the doorframe. Even in the dim light from the lamp Stinson held, William could see the deep red rims around his brother's eyes.

"You are my *only* brother." He tied the belt of the banyan securely and crossed the room. The stench of stale whiskey assaulted him before he'd even made it halfway to the door.

"Stinson, some coffee, please."

The servant nodded and departed as William propelled his brother toward the sitting room.

"Coffee? Can't understand why you drink that vile stuff, Wills. If you can't find it in your heart to give me a proper drink, could you at least order tea?"

"Coffee will sober you faster." William indicated a worn Queen Anne chair in front of the cold grate, and George tossed himself into it.

In the faint light filtering through the windows from the whale oil street lamps of St. James's, the room looked ghostly. William groped for a taper on the mantel, found one, and touched it to the coals that still glowed dimly in the grate. As he used it to light the candles in the wall sconces that flanked the fireplace, the room came into dim focus.

"Stinson's badly trained. He should have done that before haring off to the kitchen." George's voice had a superior edge that was laughable, really, considering the state he was in.

"I'm perfectly capable of lighting a lamp or two." With the taper, he ignited a branch of candles on a small side table. The room grew tolerably bright, and William took a good look at his brother for the first time since he'd arrived.

It was worse than he'd feared. George's cravat

hung limply from his neck, the end dangling almost to his substantial waist. He wore no hat and his hair stood up on end, as it was wont to do when he ran his fingers through it in a panic. The whiskey fumes wafting from him made it almost impossible to draw a fresh breath. He must have spilled a good part of the bottle on himself before drinking the rest.

Terrible waste of spirits.

William dropped onto the divan and fixed his brother with what he hoped was a steely look. "So what is it this time, George? Political disaster? Brawl in a Mayfair mews? Impending duel? I won't be your second, you know. I told you last time. Too nerve-racking."

"Worse than all that."

William felt his stomach twist as Stinson bustled in with cream and sugar. He waited to reply until the valet had placed the silver tray on the low table before George's chair and exited the room.

"Worse? Worse how, exactly?" A low pain began throbbing in his temple. George hadn't actually killed a man, had he? His brother was impulsive and reckless, but William had never known him to be violent.

George leaned back in his chair and closed his eyes. "I'm leg-shackled."

William blinked and, for a moment, was speechless.

"Married," George added helpfully. "Man and wife and all that."

For the first time, William, too, wished that Stinson was bringing something stronger than coffee. However this marriage had come about, it hadn't been proper. And that was certain to mean another long series of tasks for William, in his seemingly ceaseless career of preserving the Cates family reputation. "But how? When? I thought Lady Sarah was still in Yorkshire."

He had been startled enough when, a week ago, George had announced that he had become betrothed to a young woman from the North of England whom he had never so much as mentioned to William before. It seemed George had met the lady's father at a horse fair and had learned that the gentleman was eager to see his wellborn daughters married quickly.

William had welcomed the news of his brother's match with cautious delight. If the Wild Duke had finally decided to settle down, that could only be good news for his younger brother. If, indeed, it was true.

"Lady Sarah?" George's voice was scathing. "Good Lord, no. She's probably still up in that rotting pile on the moors. I've married Harriet."

Harriet. Good Lord. *Harriet.*

George was right. This was worse.

Without thinking, William stood and crossed the room to the small cabinet under the window. Lifting the stopper from a decanter of port, he poured himself a substantial glass.

"Now that's more like it," George said.

"This isn't for you," William snapped, returning to the divan with his drink. Fortunately, George was so preternaturally lazy that it would never occur to him to wander over to the cabinet and get his own refreshment. "Count yourself lucky that I'm giving you coffee. I should toss you into St. James's and pretend I've never seen you before."

George's eyes widened for a moment, then he laughed. "You wouldn't do that, my dear brother. I control the family purse strings. You need me."

Like a horse needs a whip, unfortunately. "If you've really done what you claim to have done, we'll need every cent in that purse just to hold our heads up in Town. Please tell me this is an elaborate prank and that you truly haven't married your mistress."

"Can't say it, Wills. The deed was done at All Saints in Chelsea three hours ago."

"At least you had the sense not to marry in Mayfair. But how did you manage to carry this off? You had no special license."

George smirked, and William knew what was coming next. "It was easy for me to procure one. No one—not even the Archbishop of Canterbury— says no to a duke."

No one says no to a duke. That was the philosophy on which George Cates, Duke of Cambermere, had based his entire existence to date. He saw no reason not to—it had served him well for more than a decade. Their father had subscribed to it as well, and when George had come into the title at the tender age of twenty-two, he had immediately begun to do his best to live up to the family legacy. No gambling den was too seedy for him, no party too outré, no companions too uncouth. His greatest joy in life was to see how far he could stray from the norms of propriety and still be welcome at the most high-in-the-instep social events. So far, he had toed the line with frightening accuracy. But this time, even he had gone too far.

"Many people are going to be saying no to you from now on," William ground out as Stinson appeared with the coffee. He nodded to the servant, who poured a large cup for George and added copious amounts of cream and sugar before handing it to the duke. George sipped it and winced.

"Vile stuff."

"If you want me to even think about helping you out of this disaster, be quiet and drink it."

George shot him a mutinous look and took another sip.

William stretched out his arm and tapped his fingers against the back of the divan. "The first thing you need to do is visit Lady Sarah."

"What on earth for?" George set the cup in its saucer with a clatter. "She has no claim on me now."

"You offered for her. She could very well sue you for breach of promise, with just cause." Such a suit would give the newspapers fine fodder for months, William realized. He could only hope he was out of the country when it all came to pass.

"She won't sue," George replied with maddening complacency. Not for the first time in his life, William suppressed an urge to slap his elder brother's face.

"And how can you be sure?"

"Can't afford it. Chit's family is in hock up to their eyes. They could not even afford to pay a solicitor to draw up the marriage settlement, which has worked to my advantage, as things have turned out. My solicitor was in the midst of drafting the papers, and I have already instructed him to destroy them. I watched myself as he laid them on the fire." George leaned back in his chair and grinned. "She has no proof of my intentions, even if she wished to sue. Which she won't."

William sat on his hands and counted to ten. "What about the ring?"

"I shall say it was simply a token of my regard. If she wants to claim it is a betrothal ring, it will be her word against mine. Whom do you think the courts will believe?"

William's heart thudded against his chest as his anger at his brother mounted. There had to be some way to make George pay for his heedlessness. William found himself eager to fight for the rights of the unknown Lady Sarah, who wasn't here to defend herself from this disaster about to befall her. "If they have published the banns, you are done for."

"They haven't. Another complete stroke of luck on my part. I didn't think it seemly for a duke's betrothal to be bruited about in some provincial church along with the marriage plans of every petty lawyer and baker in the parish, so I told them I would prefer to be married by license." He lifted his cup, sniffed it, and returned it to its saucer with a grimace. "All the *haut ton* prefers to be married by license these days. Banns are common. Harriet told me."

"And Harriet would know about the ways of polite society," William said acidly.

"Don't insult my wife," George said, his eyes narrowed. "Like it or not, she is now your sister-in-law."

"I cannot like it, but I suppose I shall have to live with it."

"Indeed you shall." George's mouth was set in a stubborn line, and William realized he would be foolish to pursue this line of conversation any further. No good could come of it, and it would only serve to antagonize his brother. There were more pressing issues to discuss.

"Despite all you have said, do you not believe you have a moral obligation to Lady Sarah?" he asked his brother. "After all, you have given her every reason to believe she is going to be the next Duchess of Cambermere."

William suppressed a groan as he realized that the woman who *had* become duchess was better known among the more outrageous men of the *ton* for her reputed skills with a few well-manipulated feathers than for her abilities as a household manager or social hostess.

"Of course, of course." George waved a hand. "I shall send her a note."

"A note? You're going to inform this innocent young woman that she is about to become the laughingstock of England by sending her a *note*?" William took a deep breath. When he spoke with his brother, he often found himself short of air.

"There is no reason for her to become a laughingstock. She has done nothing wrong. And if she has told no one of the betrothal, there will be no scandal." George eyed the cabinet under the window longingly. William ignored him. He would be damned before he'd waste one drop of his wine on his scapegrace brother.

"George, are you naive, willfully blind, or just a lackwit? Of course she will become a laughingstock. A woman who becomes engaged to a duke usually doesn't keep such news to herself. The news has probably traveled halfway around Yorkshire by now, if not farther. People will either consider her a fabulist or a jilt. Neither opinion will serve her well." With extreme difficulty, William modulated his voice. The last thing he needed was for every big-eared buck passing in the corridor to overhear this latest family scandal.

"Doesn't matter to her. Chit never comes to London. She's been moldering away in that decaying house since the day she was born, far as I can tell. And I'll be damned if I'm going to drag myself all the way up to the wilds of Yorkshire just to spare the fine feelings of some fortune-hunting miss."

"You will."

"I will not." George's voice was triumphant. "Harriet and I have plans. We are departing on our honeymoon at first light."

William tried, and failed, to keep his jaw from dropping. "And where might you be going?"

"Italy. For two months. I went to the docks and booked our passage the moment we left the church. Thought it might be best to leave Town for a few months. Allow time for the old crones at Almack's to stop wagging their tongues."

For once, George appeared to have done something sensible, William had to admit. The scandal was going to be unprecedented, and having his brother far away on the Continent could only help quell it. Of course, that left William behind to clean up the rest of the mess. As usual.

"I suppose you expect me to go to Yorkshire and break the news to Lady Sarah?"

George shrugged. "If you think it necessary."

"I do." William clenched his hands at his sides as he realized how inconvenient a trip of at least a week was going to be right now. With Boney's abdication, the foreign office had been a hive of activity. Within a few weeks, planning for a peace conference would likely begin. William had worked too hard over the last few years to be denied a choice seat at the negotiating table, simply because he wasn't present when Castlereagh decided who should comprise England's delegation. But if he didn't go to Yorkshire in an effort to repair this latest family disaster, the Cates name would likely be so tarnished that no one would want him representing his country anyway.

"Suit yourself." George stood. "So I suppose this is farewell, for now. Are you not even going to wish me happy?"

"You're the happiest creature I know, since you always do exactly what pleases you," William muttered. "Before you go, may I ask you two questions?"

George smiled, magnanimous now that he knew the worst was over. "Of course."

"What on earth inspired you to marry Harriet? You could have simply kept her in a small house in Chelsea, as sensible men do when they marry."

George looked down at the soft Aubusson carpet. "When she learned I was to marry Lady Sarah, she became somewhat . . . well . . . unbalanced."

"Meaning?"

"She threw things. Called me names. Threatened to set fire to the bed, with me in it."

"How romantic."

"She was simply distraught. I had no concept of how deeply she loved me. Marrying her seemed the only merciful thing to do."

She was likely more distraught at the thought of

losing her free rein over Cambermere House and
its deep coffers than at the thought of losing the affections of its owner, William thought. Years ago,
however, he had learned to keep such thoughts to
himself.

"Anyway, I had a few tots at my club, and when I
returned home Harriet and I shared a few more
drinks. And suddenly, it seemed an eminently practical thing to get married. She will be happy. And,
believe me, I will be happy." He smiled, an oily grin
that made William feel queasy. "Harriet knows how
to make a man delirious."

For a brief second, William reflected that the
mysterious Lady Sarah was well shot of the Duke
of Cambermere. That reminded him of his second
question.

"Where, exactly, does your now-former fiancée
live?"

As George provided somewhat garbled instruc-
tions for reaching Larkwood Manor, Lady Sarah's
family estate in Yorkshire, the gravity of the task
ahead suddenly settled on William. He would have
realized it earlier, were it not for the lateness of the
hour.

Not only did he have to tell Lady Sarah the distressing news that she would not, after all, be the
Duchess of Cambermere. And not only did he have
to dissuade her from launching a breach of
promise suit, if she had the funds to do so, but to
preserve what little was left of the family honor, he
would also have to offer for her himself.

William's throat was suddenly dry. He picked up
his glass and drained the last of the port. Within a
few minutes, George had the decency to stop talk-

ing and take his leave. As his brother stumbled out the door and back to Mayfair, William summoned Stinson to help him pack a traveling case.

What did one wear, he wondered, when proposing marriage to an utter stranger?

Rain pelted the windows of George's best traveling landau. As William had only a horse, he had taken the liberty of availing himself of his brother's extensive stables. George, after all, had left the country. The duke wouldn't need any of his horse-flesh for quite some time.

William leaned back against the squabs and marveled at how soft they were. It was astonishing, really, what a great deal of blunt could buy.

Not that he had ever resented his brother's wealth and his own comparative penury, he reflected as he closed his eyes. Not really. William had never entertained the slightest expectation of inheriting much of the Cambermere riches. The family had always settled almost all of its vast fortune on the heir. That was how it had remained a vast fortune.

Of course, their father and George had done their level best to waste it. William supposed he should be worried, but he doubted whether George—even in the company of the spendthrift Harriet—could run through enough of the family fortune to affect William's adequate stipend. As long as his share was unaffected, William really didn't care whether George spent vast sums. He was far more concerned about George's attempts to spend a much more valuable commodity: the rapidly dwindling dregs of the Cambermere reputation.

If William didn't move quickly, George's latest escapade was certain to turn into a firestorm, if it hadn't already. A week's drive away from London, it was impossible to tell whether the archbishop, a servant, or some observant dockworker had already begun spreading the news. William could only hope that it hadn't reached Yorkshire before he arrived.

The rain continued to drum on the roof. It was wearing on his nerves; the skies had not cleared once since he had left London. With the side curtains firmly buttoned to keep out the rain and cold, it was too dark to read, and he was left with deuced little to amuse himself on his journey. In a fit of boredom, he reviewed the few facts about Lady Sarah that he'd been able to glean from George.

His brother's erstwhile fiancée was the oldest daughter of Earl Glenmont, an apparent eccentric who spent most of his time building follies on the grounds of Larkwood Manor. Of the mother, George had been able to say little, as she had spent almost his entire short visit in bed with some undefined ailment. There was also an odd younger sister—"Talks of nothing but animals," George had explained—and a brother at Oxford.

On the subject of Lady Sarah herself, the duke had been almost as taciturn. "Comely enough, I suppose, if milk-and-water misses are your taste," he'd muttered. "Her family were well-born, and none of the *ton* families within a hundred miles of London would have anything to do with me. I'm two-and-thirty, it's about time I started securing the line, she seemed as likely a candidate as most, and her family needed the blunt. That's the entire story."

It wasn't much to go on. William generally preferred to have more facts about the other party before entering into delicate negotiations, but he'd proceeded on even more meager intelligence before.

So his intended was a milk-and-water miss. Not the type he would have picked, but then again, he had had little intention of picking a wife of any sort. Wives and children were just an encumbrance in his line of work. However, a family scandal was even more of an encumbrance. He sighed. There was no way to avoid offering for her. He just hoped she wasn't too unpleasant.

The carriage creaked to a stop and someone—Stinson, he supposed—leapt down from the box. He had invited his valet to ride inside the carriage with him, but Stinson had refused. Wouldn't be proper, he said, and went out to sit in the rain with John Coachman. It is true that it wouldn't have been proper, but it would have passed the time to have some company.

The carriage door opened, and Stinson stuck his fair head inside.

"According to His Grace's directions, we are only a mile or so from Larkwood," he said, removing his hat and tipping the accumulated water from the brim before replacing it on his head. "I thought you might want to have John Coachman unbutton the curtains, so that you might get a bit of a look at the place as we approach."

"Good thought, Stinson. But don't bother John

Coachman. I'll do it. Anything we can do to cut short this interminable journey is worth it, even if it saves only a minute or two." As the valet climbed back onto the box and the carriage jolted into motion once again, William unfastened the stiff leather window coverings.

The world outside the window looked most unpleasant. Rain lashed brown, deserted moors. Across one field, he spotted several gray cottages huddled around an equally gray steeple. Near the roadside, disconsolate cows munched their cud, shaking their heads occasionally to scatter drops of rain.

William thought wistfully of his warm fireside in St. James's. This was the last—absolutely the last—time he was going to extract George from a problem. On the occasion of the next disaster, his hapless brother would just have to stew in his own juices.

The carriage turned and rumbled into a rutted lane. Even the springs of the duke's top-drawer carriage couldn't insulate William completely from the bumps in the road. Good God, it was like trying to drive through a muddy field populated by industrious rabbits.

Twenty bone-jarring minutes later, the carriage had drawn up before a rambling house of weathered gray stone. Riotous brown vines, which would surely become green thickets once spring truly took hold, trailed over several windows in the eastern wing. A number of slates appeared to be missing from the roof, and one of the chimneys was wrapped in some sort of cloth, probably designed to keep out the rain. From the condition of the house, it appeared that George had not been exaggerating when he said the family was eager for the marriage settlement he had verbally promised Lady Sarah.

William squashed a sigh. Lady Sarah was not going to be pleased about his news. Not pleased at all.

Moments later, after striding through the rain and waiting longer than he would have preferred, William received an answer to his sharp knock on the door. A desiccated butler ushered him into a dim foyer, which perhaps had once been grand. Chipped black and white marble tiles stretched across a chilly expanse leading to a wide circular staircase. Portraits hung in a scattered arrangement on the walls, alternating with darker squares of paint.

He could hear no sounds of habitation. Perhaps he had come on a fool's errand. He had thought of sending a letter ahead, but he had not been able to think of a good way to explain his visit without relating the entire sordid story. However, it appeared no one was in residence.

"The family is in the back of the house," the butler said, as though he had read William's thoughts. "It faces south and is by far the warmest part of the house on damp days. May I have your name, sir, so that I may announce you?"

"I am Lord William Cates, but please do not announce me."

The butler blinked as he took William's damp greatcoat and hat.

"I would prefer a private audience with Lord

Glenmont first. Is he at home?" William handed over his gloves.

The older man shook his head. "I'm afraid not, my lord. He is in Ripon, meeting with his man of business. We do not expect him to return until very late this evening."

William suppressed a groan. He had hoped to meet the father first, to apologize for George's behavior and to ask the earl's permission to address Lady Sarah. But he could not possibly pretend he was here on a purely social call until the earl returned. He would explode from the tension.

There was nothing for it. He would have to break the news to Lady Sarah without a dress rehearsal.

"Very well. Would it be possible to meet with Lady Sarah, then?"

The butler stared at him for a moment, then seemed to regain his power of speech. "As you are soon to be her relative, I suppose there is no harm in that."

"It need not be completely private. In fact, I would prefer to have a servant about, for propriety's sake." A maid or footman might come in handy if his brother's betrothed dissolved into floods of tears at the news.

By heaven, he was not looking forward to this.

"Very well, my lord. Please, have a seat in the drawing room. I will send Lady Sarah to you directly."

The butler opened a set of double doors on one side of the foyer and ushered William inside. It was clear that the drawing room was rarely used. Dust was thick on the side tables, and a stale smell lingered in the upholstery. After opening the blue

velvet drapes swathing the windows, the butler motioned a young footman into the room.

William suppressed a shiver. It felt colder in this
room than it had been in the carriage. It seemed
that he had not been warm for more than ten minutes together since leaving London a week ago.

The footman wandered about the room, lighting
candles and stoking the fire in the grate. Moments
later, apparently satisfied that he had done everything in his power to make the room welcoming,
he retired to a small chair in the shadows on the
other side of the fireplace.

The lad could not be more than ten years old,
William realized. He wondered just what the child
would do if he did indeed behave improperly toward Lady Sarah during their meeting—not that he
had any intention of doing so, of course.

He did not have long to ponder the question, as
at that moment the door to the drawing room
opened. He rose and turned toward the entrance
to get a good first look at his future wife.

When she swept in, his first thought was that
George was even more of a fool than William had
always thought. It was instantly apparent that Lady
Sarah was no milk-and-water miss.

She was slight and small, but she radiated energy
like a well-stoked fire. Her cheeks were rosy, her
eyes snapped with intelligence, and she strode into
the room with confidence. What appeared to be a
luxurious mane of chestnut hair was coiled at the
back of her head in a simple, unfashionable style,
and her day dress was similarly plain. He had seen
many simpering young women during his years in

Town, and Lady Sarah bore no resemblance to any of them.

"Lord William!" she cried, extending her hands toward him. "His Grace mentioned he had a brother, of course, but I had no idea that you planned to do us the honor of a visit. What a pleasure to make your acquaintance! I am Lady Sarah Harrison."

He took her hands and nodded. "The pleasure is all mine, my lady." With difficulty, he kept his voice calm and neutral. It had been hard enough to contemplate his distasteful errand when the recipient of his bad news had been an unknown cipher. It was doubly difficult now. "I apologize for not sending word in advance."

"What brings you to Yorkshire on such a damp, dull day?" she asked as she took a seat on a worn green velvet settee and motioned him to return to his chair. Her smile was warm and genuine.

He felt like a servant sent out to do away with an unwanted litter of kittens. His stomach twisted as he sat down and looked into her trusting face. There was no point delaying the worst. "I have come with most unpleasant news, Lady Sarah."

Her eyes widened. "Is it the duke? Is he ill? Is he . . . dead?"

He should be, William thought grimly, for putting his brother and his betrothed through this deuced awkward meeting. "No." He took a deep breath and spread his hands out on his knees. "He is, however, married. To another."

The color drained from her cheeks.

TWO

Breathe, Sarah told herself. *You know what happens when you forget to breathe.*

She drew in a deep, noisy gulp of air.

"Are you all right, Lady Sarah?" Lord William asked, leaning forward.

She nodded, willing her breath to return to normal. She would not—would *not*—swoon like some ridiculous heroine in a Gothic novel.

"I am well. Thank you for asking," she said in a surprisingly normal voice. The chill that had gripped her when Lord William first made his announcement was quickly receding. Beads of sweat popped out on her forehead, and her hands began to tremble.

This cannot be happening. Everything was arranged. All our debts would be paid off. Now I—we—have nothing. No dignity. No prospects. And, apparently, no husband.

"Does your brother make a habit of offering for unmarried women?" she asked in an attempt at levity, hoping to disguise her growing mortification. "It must be a terrible inconvenience to his wife."

Lord William blinked at her question before understanding dawned in his eyes. "He is only newly married. A week ago yesterday, in fact."

So he had married this other person after offering for her, Sarah realized. Perhaps he had rethought his decision to join the Harrison clan. He wouldn't be the first gentleman to have done so, although he was the only one to have progressed as far as an actual offer before crying off.

She nodded. Feeling as though she were dreaming a terrible dream, she twisted the Cambermere emerald betrothal ring from her finger and handed it to the duke's brother.

"Well, no matter how long he has been married, it would be inappropriate for me to continue to wear this."

Lord William looked down at the gem for a moment or two, then closed his fingers over it and shook his head. "Lady Sarah, you are taking this sordid news very well. If you would like to speak out against my brother, please feel free to do so. Believe me, I have treated him to more than a few choice words about his behavior myself."

Sarah shook her head. "It would change nothing. Whom has he married, if I may ask?"

Lord William ran a finger around the edge of his expertly tied neckcloth, pulling it gently away from his throat. He had a very nice throat, she thought. It went well with the rest of him. The duke might be the heir to the family title, but it appeared that Lord William—with his tousled dark hair and eyes as green as the emerald he held in his palm—was the heir to the fabled Cambermere looks.

"His wife is the former Miss Harriet Partridge." He raised his eyebrows, as if expecting her to recognize the name. It meant nothing to her.

"I wish them happiness." She wished them nothing of the sort, but the well-worn phrase was the only thing she could think of to utter that was not a high-pitched scream loud enough to frighten the horses in the far-off stable. "Our betrothal seemed too good to be true, in any case," she muttered without thinking.

"Lady Sarah, please do not blame yourself. My brother has many admirable qualities—although, to be honest, I cannot think of a single one at the moment—but he is notoriously impulsive and careless of others' feelings. My deepest apologies, on behalf of my family, for the hurt and embarrassment he has caused you."

She nodded, and struggled to speak around the lump in her throat. Lord William appeared to be as kind as his brother was thoughtless. "Embarrassment, yes, but not hurt. It was not a love match. I am certainly under no illusion that His Grace was besotted with me."

Lord William nodded. "Nor you with him, I gather."

Sarah suppressed a wince. Was it that obvious that she had leapt at the chance to marry the first wealthy gentleman to ask her, without considering his character? She supposed that the speed of their betrothal was all the evidence one would need to come to that conclusion.

"I found Lord Cambermere charming, but that was not the reason I accepted his offer." She sighed. "I suppose it is better to have learned he is a scoundrel before the wedding rather than after. I assume that this impulsive and careless reputation you mentioned is the reason that he has not married before, or married someone closer to home?"

The dark-haired gentleman nodded. "His sobriquet is 'the Wild Duke.' Despite the fact that an exalted title usually attracts crowds of ambitious young ladies and their equally starry-eyed mamas, only the most desperate families were willing to let their daughters be seen in his company. If I had known that he had come all the way to Yorkshire in search of a wife, I would have taken the time to warn the local gentry." A small, sheepish smile played about his lips.

Such a warning would have saved a great deal of trouble, Sarah reflected as the depth of her predicament became clear. As well as contending with the financial disaster the duke's defection would bring about, she would need to start writing letters to her friends and relatives, informing them of the embarrassing news.

A thought suddenly occurred to her. She could appeal to the courts, try to regain something from this debacle. But as soon as the idea crossed her mind, she dismissed it. Months ago, the family had stopped buying tea. They barely had enough ready cash to buy sugar. They certainly would not have enough money to pay a barrister, particularly for a case there was a very good chance she would lose, since it rested largely on hearsay.

"Much as I should like redress, you may rest assured that I shall not sue for breach of promise," Lady Sarah informed her guest. "As your brother has no doubt informed you, we have not the means to pursue such a suit."

Lord William nodded. "I tried to get George to live up to the spirit of his agreement, but he refused. Unfortunately, he is now abroad, so I cannot further persuade him to be honorable. I know for a fact that he will simply tear up any imploring letters I send. When he doesn't want to deal with an issue, he simply ignores it." He leaned forward. "However, I should like to make amends, from my own pocket."

Sarah shook her head. "That would not be fair. This disaster is not of your making. Besides, the amount of money it would take to repair the fortunes of my family is far beyond anything I could ask of you." There was no sense begging Lord William to throw his own money into the bottomless well of their debt. It would not make the slightest bit of difference. And she would die before she felt the slightest obligation to any relative of the Duke of Cambermere, even one as kind as Lord William appeared to be. She would find a way out of this disaster on her own.

An awkward silence fell between them. Sarah heard the wind whistling through the cracks in the front window, and she moved to observe the progress of the storm.

It had become a nasty spring squall. The branches of the linden trees lining the lane twisted in the gale, and almost all the light had disappeared from the late afternoon sky.

Much as she wanted to put as much distance as possible between herself and the Cates family, she could not send Lord William back out into such a tempest. The nearest inn was fifteen miles distant, and on a night like this, there was no guarantee it would have any rooms to let. She turned from the window to regard her guest.

"Lord William, I deeply appreciate the time and

effort you have expended to travel to Yorkshire to bring me this news in person," she said, her voice sounding stiff and foolish even in her own ears. "The least I can do is offer you our hospitality for the evening. The weather is growing worse, and you are most welcome to take shelter here. The accommodations are not luxurious, but I believe we have at least one guest room whose roof doesn't leak."

He smiled faintly and glanced at the window. His left hand clenched the arm of the worn Sheraton settee. It was obvious that he would not choose to spend a night under the Harrison roof if he could help it. "I hate to take advantage of your kind nature, but I believe you are right. It is not a fit night for man nor beast outside. Thank you for the invitation."

"You are most welcome. Would you like to come and meet the rest of the family? As I presume Jones told you, my father is away." She moved toward the door, glad that this awkward interview was at an end. Perhaps she could bring him to the south salon, introduce him to the rest of the family, and flee to her room before anyone had the chance to ask her any questions—or before she began to cry like a green girl.

What would become of them now? Her father was in Ripon negotiating with their man of business in the optimistic hope that the Duke of Cambermere was about to settle a most generous amount on her. It was probably too late to stop him. Would he make promises they could not keep?

"Lady Sarah?" Lord William's voice cut into her thoughts. With a guilty flush, she realized he had been saying her name for several moments as she contemplated her increasingly bleak future.

She forced herself to return to the distressing present. "Yes?"

"Before we meet your family, I have one last thing I would like to say." He tugged at his neckcloth again, in what she already recognized as a characteristic gesture of discomfort.

What could possibly be as awful as the news he had already given her? As her breathing quickened, she forced her hands to stay still and her voice to stay calm. "Certainly, my lord. Please speak freely."

He looked her in the eye. "Would you do me the honor, Lady Sarah, of becoming *my* wife?"

She stared at him as though he had suggested they scamper off to York and buy commissions in the army together. What on earth was he thinking?

"Unfortunately, due to the provisions of my father's will, I have a much smaller income than George does. It is adequate but not exceptional." He spoke in even, measured tones, as though this were a speech he had rehearsed in his carriage on the way to Yorkshire. "As a result, I cannot guarantee that I can offer you the same sort of financial arrangement my brother promised you, but I can do my best to negotiate one."

When she said nothing, he seemed compelled to offer up further incentives. "If nothing else, marrying me will allow you to save face in the eyes of society." He sat back in his chair and eyed her. Clearly, he had finished outlining all the advantages of the match.

Hot humiliation crept through Sarah's veins, making her blush and turning her stomach. It had been bad enough to accept one offer based on financial reward. But to accept one based on pity would be intolerable.

"I appreciate your kindness, Lord William, but you do not need to pity me. It is through no fault of my own that your brother has cried off." She had to believe that. She *had* to. Otherwise, she would dissolve in a heap on the floor in front of this man, and then his condescension would know no bounds.

"Lady Sarah, I am not making my offer out of pity. You would be doing my family an enormous favor, by helping me save what little honor my scapegrace brother has not managed to squander." He favored her with a boyish smile, and then she did forget to breathe for a moment.

From their few minutes' acquaintance, Lady Sarah knew that Lord William was sober, proper, and more than a little stuffy. But his tilted grin made him look as rakish as the pictures she had seen of Lord Byron. That smile definitely did not run in the Cates family. No expression that had ever crossed the Duke of Cambermere's face had affected her so.

She brought her attention back to more serious matters and considered Lord William's argument. She did not want to leave him in any difficulty. He seemed a nice gentleman, after all.

You have difficulties of your own, she reminded herself. Other women might have the freedom to be swayed by a charming smile. She needed to find a husband with plenty of ready blunt, and it appeared that Lord William—for all his evident attributes—could not provide her with a fortune.

She suspected that he was prepared to be persuasive, and *that* she could not bear. Any minute now, her facade was going to crack. She needed to end this interview quickly. And the only way she could think of to dissuade him in short order was to be rude.

"Thank you very much for your kind offer," she said slowly. "But your family has created this dilemma. It is no concern of mine how you extricate yourself from it."

Every word was painful. If she had had only her own wishes to consider, she would have at least contemplated Lord William's offer. Certainly, he was by far the most appealing of the motley string of suitors who had appeared at her door, most of them courtesy of her father's haphazard matchmaking efforts. She doubted that anyone half as charming would appear on her doorstep again.

Remember the debt. Other women could afford to marry for love. Lady Sarah Harrison, daughter of the sweet but spendthrift Earl Glenmont, was not one of them. Much as it galled her, she had to hunt down a fortune. She moved toward the door.

"I am afraid I must decline, with gratitude," she said, trying to take the sting out of her earlier words. She reached for the doorknob and prayed that he would let her leave without further argument.

As usual, lately, her prayer went unanswered. "Wait, Lady Sarah."

She forced herself to look at him. His face was mottled, and the charming smile had disappeared. His mouth was set in a hard, thin line. Botheration—she had offended him. That was the last thing she'd wanted to do.

"Please. I ask you to reconsider."

She closed her eyes. Why was he making this so difficult? He had done more than propriety required, and she was giving him the perfect excuse to walk away. The more he tried to save her, the more awkward the conversation would become. Desperately, she searched for something suitably cutting that would wound him enough that he would let her go. She hated to hurt him, but if she didn't escape this room quickly, she feared she would scream.

"Thank you for your persistence, Lord William, but my answer remains no." She gritted her teeth. "I have been affianced to a duke. Will I not look desperate if I leap immediately into an alliance with a younger son?"

She quelled a spurt of remorse at her cruel, false jibe. Titles meant nothing to her—she would have married the coachman's son if he had a fortune at his command.

Lord William greeted her question with silence. With relief, she realized that she had finally deflected him. She yanked open the door, wishing only to rush upstairs and hide herself in her room. But his next words stilled her feet.

"I would think someone in your situation could ill afford to be so selective. I may be your last, best hope. Do reconsider, my lady." His voice was strained and glacial.

If he hoped to change her mind by matching her cruelty with his own, he was mistaken. She needed no reminding that her situation was desperate.

Hadn't she tossed and turned in bed night after night before her father's fortuitous meeting with the duke, wondering how on earth she was going to repair her family's fortunes with the paltry means at her disposal: a respected family name, a crumbling family home, an unremarkable face and figure, and a list of creditors as long as the Domesday Book?

She was sorry she had wounded his pride, but he was *not* going to shame her into making a decision that would see her family lose their house and their reputation.

"You may indeed be my best hope. You may even be my last hope. But I have no choice in the matter but to take my chances that you are not." Without looking back, she slipped through the open door. "I will have Jones show you to your room. Please excuse me. I feel a megrim coming on."

As she climbed the main staircase two at a time, she berated herself. A *megrim*? When in her life had she ever used such a missish excuse to extract herself from a situation?

That was the least of her concerns at the moment, however. As she reached the second-floor landing and hurried down the corridor toward her room, she reviewed the situation. Within three months, as far as she could tell, the Harrisons would be forced to rent out Larkwood if they could not lay their hands on some ready cash.

She envisioned the scene: a farm wagon piled with the few possessions so decrepit that they could not be sold to pay the debt. Her father humiliated, her mother uncomprehending. Her sister sent to serve as governess or lady's companion in some de-

manding household. Her brother forced to leave
Oxford. The whole family as vagabonds, moving
from one relation's home to another, dependent always on charity.

No. Sarah would fight to her last breath before
that scenario came to pass.

Finally, she reached the sanctuary of her room.
Pushing open the door, she slipped inside and
closed it behind her. As she looked around her one
remaining sanctuary, she felt her shoulders slump.
Suddenly, she was almost unbearably weary. She
had been fighting this battle for so long.

She dragged herself to the pretty blue wing chair,
drawn up close to a grate that spilled out a faint
warmth. She dropped into the seat and pulled her
feet up beneath her, as she had done since she was
a child, much to her mother's distress at such unladylike manners. Tucking her chin into the soft
velvet of the chair's wing, she let her mind roam
free.

Perhaps she should have accepted Lord William's
offer. True, he was a bit of a stuffed shirt. Certainly,
he was more bookish and mild than his flamboyant
brother. On the other hand, he seemed principled
and kind. After their one brief meeting, she already
sensed that *he* would be unlikely to elope with one
woman when he was already promised to another.
That was a decided advantage.

Lord William's income might be modest, but it
was more than she was likely to see from any other
man in the next several months. Perhaps he might
even have been able to convince his brother to provide a handsome wedding settlement.

Don't be a widgeon. You could not possibly marry him.

Unless he succeeded in extracting a settlement as large as the one the duke originally promised you, such a marriage would do you little good. Your family would still be just a thread's width from disgrace.

So she had done the right thing in rejecting him, she reassured herself. Her main regret was that she had done the deed so gracelessly. If only Lord William hadn't been so sympathetic when he made his offer. "Marrying me will allow you to save face in the eyes of society," he had said.

A stranger was willing to commit himself to her for life, just to help her avoid embarrassment? Such a grand gesture implied that he thought her humiliation so monumental that only a huge sacrifice could redeem it. A wave of hot shame washed over her.

Sarah dug her chin more deeply into the upholstery. For years, she had tried to conquer her senseless pride. Heaven knew, the Harrison family had precious little to be proud of at the moment. But some days, her sense of herself and her family's legacy was the only thing that stood between her and despair.

That pride had been her undoing this afternoon, however. Mixed with fear that she would start crying, pride had led her to make those horrible remarks to Lord William. She groaned as she remembered what she had said. The gentleman had traveled halfway across England to help fix a situation he had had no hand in creating, and she had repaid him with barbs.

Understandably, he had responded in kind. *Your last, best hope.* Each word had pricked her like a tiny, sharp sword. Without knowing it, he had put her deepest fear into words. She had failed in her final effort to gain respectability, and soon she would be an object of pity for all and sundry.

Poor Sarah. Jilted by a duke, and not even a plump dowry to recommend her. Who will have her now? She could almost hear the voice of Mrs. Chawton, the vicar's sharp-tongued wife, in her head.

The tears that had been pricking at the back of Sarah's eyes since Lord William's startling announcement of the duke's marriage now spilled down her cheeks. She scrubbed at her face with the back of her hand.

Crying would solve nothing. She had thrown away one chance at marriage, and there was nothing left for it now but to try to find another willing husband with a heavy purse. Quickly.

But first, to ease her conscience, she would have to apologize to Lord William.

William punched the thin pillow and settled back down into the lumpy bed. Sleep, however, continued to elude him. He hadn't had a decent night's rest since George had pounded on his door a week ago.

Sighing, he tossed back the threadbare coverlet and got out of bed. A small lamp still glowed on the mantel. He crossed the room, picked up the lamp, and carried it to a small table by the window, where he had placed the biography of Napoleon that had diverted him during the long journey north.

He opened the thick volume and squinted at the words marching across the page. Perhaps a few minutes' reading would relax him enough to sleep.

He found it almost impossible to concentrate, however. As a gust of wind rattled the window behind him, his skin prickled. He began scanning the room for his banyan before remembering that he had advised Stinson not to pack the bulky garment. It was spring, after all. He hadn't thought he'd need it.

But spring in Yorkshire was a different creature altogether from the softer season in the south. The April chill here reminded him of the spring he had once spent in Stockholm negotiating a series of minor treaties. Stockholm was a delightful place in the summer, though, and he assumed that Yorkshire was the same. Why else would anyone live here? From what little he had seen, the landscape had little enough to recommend it. He knew some writers waxed poetic about these deserted moors, but he had little taste for them. The sunny ports of the Adriatic were more his style.

The window trembled again as unseen raindrops crackled against it. The gooseflesh on his forearms intensified. With a sigh, he crossed the room, extracted his coat from the wardrobe, and shrugged into it. It likely looked ridiculous with his nightclothes, but he would rather be warm than stylish, particularly when no one was about to see him.

He returned to the chair and his book. Now that he was warm, he fully expected to become absorbed in the volume. But after reading less than a page, he found his attention returning once again to the subject that had preoccupied him all evening—Lady Sarah.

He could still see her eyes, blue as cold lake water in her pale face, as he delivered his final jibe before she fled the room. Raising his hand to his face, he closed his eyes and pinched the bridge of his nose. He had handled that entire encounter very poorly. Such ham-handed tactics were sometimes useful in breaking stalemates in difficult diplomatic situations, but his approach had been entirely wrong for such a delicate affair. What had he been thinking?

Well, she had goaded him with that remark about younger sons. That had been devilish rude. He supposed she didn't move about much in polite society. George had said she rarely ventured far from home. It was just as well she had turned down his offer. If he had to have a wife, he needed one with a bit of tact.

Still, it was odd that he had reacted so sharply to her unmannerly comments. He usually had a thicker skin about such things. She had said nothing that wasn't the absolute truth: he had neither the name nor the fortune that George did. He had long ago accepted that he would be a minor star in the firmament of society, in which George was a famous constellation. And by and large, he had been happy with that status. He preferred to lie low, to observe life from the sidelines rather than from the center.

He had come here to console her, not to antagonize her. So why had her remark spurred him to such viciousness? He had no idea.

After she had left the room, he had not had the stomach to meet the rest of the family. It was cowardly, yes, but he suspected that he would be less likely to deepen the muddle he had made of things if he could just stay in his room and gather his thoughts before the next encounter with any other member of the Harrison clan. Besides, he had reasoned, if he made himself scarce, it would give Lady Sarah the chance to explain her side of the story to her relations.

So when Jones had arrived to escort him to the back of the house, he had said that he would prefer instead to be shown to his room to freshen up. The butler accepted this logical request without question. And when William did not make an appearance downstairs again that evening, it appeared that no one cared.

In the morning, he would try to make amends with Lady Sarah, pay his respects and say his farewells to her family, and put this entire unpleasant episode behind him. By tomorrow evening, he would be partway back to London, and far from Larkwood Manor and Lady Sarah.

Truly, he had had a fortunate escape. With her quick tongue and apparently odd family, his brother's former fiancée would have done him no credit as a wife. So why did he feel so uneasy?

He had done all that propriety required, he reminded himself. Hell, he had done *more* than propriety required. He had practically begged Lady Sarah to accept him, even though the last thing he wanted was to be leg-shackled. His work meant that he spent far more time in foreign capitals than in England. It was no life for a woman, being dragged from Vienna to Versailles to Verona. He made do with simple lodgings well within his means when he was abroad. But if he were to bring a wife along, expenses would rise. And if there were children—

He pinched the bridge of his nose again. The expenses and the difficulties would multiply exponentially.

No, he had put himself at considerable risk and inconvenience just by offering for Lady Sarah. The fact that he had upset her in the process could not undo that fact. He had fulfilled the dictates of Society, done his best to clear up George's latest debacle. He should be able to sleep the sleep of the just. If only he could forget that stricken look on Lady Sarah's face when he had pointed out that she could not afford to be choosy.

He sighed and grabbed his book again. His behavior had been poor, but if there was one thing he had learned on the diplomatic circuit, it was to avoid regrets. They served only to hamper one's future progress.

Thus resolved, he opened the book and began to read about Boney's leadership of the Army of Italy.

THREE

Sometime later, William awakened with a painful twist in his neck.

He looked down to realize he had fallen asleep in the chair by the window. What a picture he would have presented to any servant who had happened to disturb him! With his mouth agape and his coat rumpled, he looked more like a Whitechapel beggar than a diplomat.

Stinson would be appalled at the state of his coat. With luck, his valet had had time to press the other coat in his traveling case. Not that it mattered greatly, as the garment would just become wrinkled again during today's long journey south.

What time was it, anyway? The light behind the draperies seemed dim. Perhaps he could enjoy another hour or two of sleep before departing.

He glanced at the clock on the mantel, which showed that it was just a few minutes after nine. That couldn't possibly be right; the room was dim as midnight.

He crossed the room and twitched open the burgundy curtains, suppressing a cough as a cloud of dust assailed his nostrils. Outside the window, it was daylight, but just barely. The sky, unbelievably, was even darker than it had been the day before, with thick black clouds edged with sickly green. Rain lashed the fields, which were littered with tree branches and other detritus. Low in the distance, William heard the rumble of thunder. Glancing toward the main road, he saw neither horse nor carriage.

Damn. He was trapped in this blasted provincial backwater with a woman who likely despised him, with reason. And every day that passed was another day he could not be involved in the negotiations arising from Napoleon's abdication.

Bloody hell.

At that moment, he heard a scratch at the door. He called out and Stinson entered, carrying a steaming ewer and a spotless jacket of blue superfine. Well, at least one thing was going right this morning.

"I see you've observed the traveling conditions, my lord," the servant remarked.

"Indeed, I have, if one can even contemplate travel on such a grim day."

"I would not advise it. Lord Glenmont apparently arrived home very late last night, having been delayed by several hours when his carriage swerved off the slick road into a ditch. It was fortunate that the axle did not break."

William nodded. "The rain today appears even more fierce than yesterday." He let the curtain fall and rubbed his hands together. "There is nothing for it but to endure, I suppose." The enforced extension of his stay at Larkwood Manor would at least give him ample opportunity to make amends to Lady Sarah, he reflected. He could not undo

George's mistakes, but he could at least apologize for his own thoughtless remarks. That was something.

Half an hour later, freshly shaved and dressed, William made his way downstairs. The clatter of dishes and the hum of conversation toward the back of the house led him to the breakfast room, where a decidedly odd party was enjoying the morning meal.

When William entered, the room fell silent, save for the soft clinks of silverware dropping to the damask-covered table.

At the head of the table sat a gray-haired gentleman whom William assumed to be Sarah's father. The earl was wearing a damp, mud-spattered jacket, and flecks of sodden leaves clung to his wispy locks. Neither fact appeared to distract him from his determined attack on a huge platter of eggs, toast, blood pudding, and sausages.

Where did the man put it all? William wondered. He was as thin as a rail.

The woman at the other end of the table was as portly as the earl was spindly. With effort, William quelled thoughts of Jack Sprat and his wife.

The lady who was likely the countess had pulled her chair some distance from the table to accommodate the enormous panniers that spread on both sides of her skirts. She was sampling her meal with dainty bites, doubtless to avoid disturbing the thick coating of white powder that all but disguised her face. The closest William had ever been to such an ensemble was a portrait of his grandmother, which hung in the foyer of Cambermere House and had been painted half a century earlier. How very odd.

The Harrisons were evidently given to bold sartorial statements, if the young man serving himself from the chafing dishes on the sideboard was any indication. His jacket of canary yellow silk capped peacock blue pantaloons. When he turned from the sideboard, plate in hand, William spotted a large quizzing glass dangling from his neck by a scarlet ribbon.

"Well, you must be Lord William!" cried the youth in a high-pitched voice. "Didn't know if we were going to spy you or not! Come in, come in, sit down. I'm Chadwick, Sarah's brother." Setting his plate on the table with a clatter, he rushed toward William, holding out a soft hand.

Bemused, William shook it. "I am pleased to meet you, my lord. I confess I am surprised, however. I understood from my brother that you are studying at Oxford."

Chadwick waved a careless hand. "Nominally, yes. I came back for Easter and just haven't found it in my heart yet to return. Too much fun here. Besides, if I wait a week or two, I will be able to travel with a friend who is in possession of a fine carriage and team."

Oxford must have become much more sedate in the years since William had attended, if an isolated estate in Yorkshire could be deemed more exciting. But he refrained from comment.

"Let me introduce my parents," the youth continued, brimming over with nervousness or high spirits, William couldn't tell which. "This is my father, Lord Glenmont."

Slowly, the older man stood and offered his hand to his guest. "Lord William. Welcome. If you plan to stay today, I must show you about the estate. A few projects under way you might find interesting. Hardly get the chance to show anyone, these days. So few people stop by." A scrap of dried greenery drifted from his hair to the floor. He ignored it, nodded briefly at William, and returned to his plate.

Chadwick seemed to find nothing untoward in the earl's odd greeting, as he continued his introductions. "And this is my mother, Lady Glenmont."

The rotund lady nodded. "Good morning, Lord William," she said in a low, pleasant voice. "I am pleased to make your acquaintance. The circumstances are not the best, of course, but that is not your fault."

He flashed her a genuine smile of gratitude.

"And finally, please meet my sister, Lady Hester," Chadwick said.

Sister? What sister? William glanced around in surprise until he spotted a slim woman dressed in gray, lingering by the tea tray on the far side of the room. She had not moved or made a sound since he had entered the room, he was certain.

As pale and quiet as her sister was vibrant and vivid, Lady Hester resembled nothing so much as a hare cornered by a fox. The hand holding a flowered china cup shook as she dropped him a small curtsey.

"Good . . . good morning, m'lord," she murmured, before placing cup and saucer on the sideboard and scampering from the room.

"Hester's not much for people," Chadwick explained.

Evidently.

William glanced around the room. Lady Sarah was nowhere in evidence, although there were two used plates on the table—a half-full one that probably belonged to Lady Hester, and an empty one.

"Where might I find Lady Sarah?"

His inquiry was met with dull silence. Had she told them all to keep him away from her? Understandable, but it would not suit his purposes. He truly wanted to put things right with her.

Chadwick looked at his mother, who looked at her husband. Lord Glenmont continued to eat with gusto. As the silence lengthened, however, the earl looked up.

"Barn," he said with a vague wave toward the back of the house. Then he returned his attention to his meal.

"If you seek Sally out, take an umbrella," the countess piped up.

"You might want to wait until it stops raining," Chadwick suggested. "You won't want to soil that jacket. Demmed fine cut, that. Weston?"

William nodded, distracted. What on earth could Lady Sarah be doing in the barn on a day like this? Surely she wasn't contemplating a ride?

Probably petting the horses or playing with some barnyard kittens, he decided as he thanked his hosts, left the breakfast room, and collected his greatcoat and hat from the antique butler.

It was quite remarkable, he thought as he circled the house and crossed the stable yard toward the barn, that someone as seemingly normal and self-possessed as Lady Sarah had sprung from such an odd family. Then again, he liked to think of himself as the white sheep of the Cambermere connection. Family does not make a man, he had told himself often enough.

Rain stung his face and drilled through his coat as he strode toward the dilapidated barn on the far side of the yard. The main doors were closed against the elements, so he ventured to a small side door, lifted the latch, and entered.

It took a moment for his eyes to adjust to the gloom. The air was dusty and surprisingly dry, given the tempest outside. The earthy smells of hay and horses assailed his nostrils.

A groom sat on a bench in the corner, mending tack.

"Ye lookin' for Lady Sarah, m'lord?" he asked.

William nodded.

"Ye'll find her at the far end of the barn." He pointed, then returned to his bits of leather.

William strode up the main aisle, then paused as a horse whickered softly. He turned to spy a tired-looking roan mare. She was almost the only horse in the place, aside from several elderly workhorses.

"Hello, beautiful," he said, wishing he had a lump of sugar to offer her. She looked as though she could use it.

At the end of the row of stalls was another large doorway, likely the entrance to the carriage room. He strolled toward it and listened. Instead of laughter, as one might expect if Lady Sarah was amusing herself with a barn cat, he heard a high, thin whistle, followed by the sharp clink of metal on metal.

What the devil?

Approaching the entrance on light feet, he peered around the worn wooden door.

In the light filtering in from a dirty window at the back of the barn, he saw two slight figures circling each other. Ugly leather caps covered their heads, and both wore plain white shirts, buff breeches, and boots. Each held a foil. And, as the shirt and snug inexpressibles clearly revealed, the one on the left was not male.

As William came to this realization, the lithe figure executed a swift parry, knocking her opponent's foil firmly sideways. Even more quickly, the blade sliced through the air and thudded as it connected with the young man's leather-sheathed midriff.

With relief, William realized that the combatants were fighting with fleurets. The leather buttons on the tips of the foils would protect them both from serious injury, thank God.

In appalled fascination, he watched as the figure who was clearly Lady Sarah danced away from her opponent's determined attack. Perhaps William had been too swift in deeming his brother's former fiancée the white sheep of her family. A woman who fenced? Her transgression wasn't quite in the same league as that of a duke who married his mistress, William conceded, but it was certainly odd.

For about a minute, she succeeded in eluding her opponent's thrusts, but then the young man's fleuret scored a direct hit on her shoulder.

"Touché," she cried, with a delighted laugh. "You're improving every day, Sam."

"You are still more than my match. You seem very swift this morning."

"I have a great deal of bad humor to work out."
She shifted and launched what was surely a feint,
aiming for Sam's well-defended right thigh.

William imagined that most of that bad humor
was directed at himself or at George, and he could
hardly fault her for that. It was rather unladylike
of her to mention it, of course. Then again, she
wasn't looking particularly womanly at the minute.

The young man took Lady Sarah's bait, execut-
ing an octave parry to protect his right torso and
riposting. She immediately parried his riposte and
executed a counter-riposte.

She was incredibly fast. Even in Angelo's fencing
rooms in Soho, she would be a worthy competitor.
The fact that her technique was more fluid than
most men's—coupled with the alluring picture she
made in her flowing shirt and skin-tight inexpressibles—would make her a particularly distracting
opponent. How could a man focus on her footwork
and bladework when she displayed her legs to such
unseemly effect?

Perhaps George had been wise to cry off after all.
Fencing was no hobby for any woman who aspired
to be the Duchess of Cambermere. George had already done enough to attract the wrong sort of
attention to the family, without adding a dueling
duchess to the mix.

"Would you like to join us, Lord William, or
would you prefer to lurk in the shadows for the rest
of the morning?"

With a start, he realized that they had ceased
fighting and were both staring at him. Sam had removed his cap and was blushing furiously.

"And who might you be?" William asked him,

mainly to cover up his own embarrassment at having been caught observing the combatants.

"Sam Detlor, m'lord," he said, tugging his forelock. "I'm a groom here. Lady Sarah and me, we practice sometimes. Her father says 'tis fine, but mine says 'tis improper. She insisted this morning, m'lord."

William nodded. He had no grudge against the lad. "I agree with your father. It is highly irregular." As soon as he spoke, he could have bitten off his tongue. Just because he thought Lady Sarah's hobby hoydenish, there had been no need to say so. Judging by the way she had just crossed her arms on her chest, he had antagonized her. "But you did right to obey your mistress's wishes," he added hastily.

The groom shrugged. "I'll be getting back to work now, m'lady," he said, laying his cap on a hay bale in the corner and beginning to sidle away.

"No, Sam, wait." Lady Sarah's tone brooked no argument. "Do you fence, Lord William?"

He blinked. She couldn't be about to suggest—? "Yes." He spoke quickly in an effort to block the most improper picture that had taken shape in his mind's eye. "I take instruction with Angelo. In London."

Her eyes, barely visible through the slit in her mask, seemed to widen. "You are fortunate. My father had the good luck to learn from Angelo's father many years ago, but all I have is access to the elder Angelo's manuals."

So that was how she'd learned. That, and perhaps some instruction from her deucedly odd parent. Well, it was not for him to judge. Amusements in this northern backwater were likely rather scarce. What harm was it, really, if she chose to amuse herself by dancing about the barn in boys' clothing?

"How did you come by your costume?" he asked, more to make conversation than because he really wanted to know.

"Chadwick. These are old garments he has outgrown."

William nodded but couldn't think of another polite thing to say.

"So, are you going to demonstrate your skills for me?" Her voice was laced with good-natured laughter. If she felt embarrassed at being caught in such odd circumstances, she was doing a very good job of disguising it.

"By fighting Sam?" Even as he asked it, he knew that was not what she intended.

"No. Sam is just learning. It wouldn't be fair. I'm asking you to engage me."

He thought of reminding her that he had made just such an offer yesterday, only to be rejected as a worthless second son, but decided it would not be politic to mention that. "That would not be proper, Lady Sarah, and you know it." Surely she had some concept of the dictates of Society?

"Who would see? Only Sam—he can serve as chaperon—and he won't breathe a word. Will you, Sam?"

"No." The youth shook his head, his eyes wide as a startled puppy's. William wouldn't bet money on the boy's vow not to share this juicy story, among the servants at least. That was just what he needed circulating around Yorkshire—a tawdry tale of him fencing with Earl Glenmont's daughter.

"Lady Sarah, be reasonable. It is scandalous even for me to see you in such unconventional clothing." He knew he sounded like a prig, but he couldn't help himself. He was beginning to heartily regret coming to the barn in the first place.

"No one will care." She shrugged. "My family, as you may have noticed, aren't sticklers for propriety. They know I have already turned down your offer. And they know as well as I do that I must make a lucrative match." Her voice was tinged with bitterness. "Believe me, no one at Larkwood will force a marriage, no matter how compromising our circumstances appear."

The tone of defeat in her voice reminded him of just what a precarious position George had placed her in. If his brother had described the family's financial situation accurately, the Harrisons were very close to penury. Lady Sarah's chances of marrying well had been slight before she'd met George. They were almost nonexistent now that she had become his jilt. There had to be some way William could make reparation for the damage George had done. But first, he had to extricate himself from this bizarre situation.

"Be that as it may . . ." How could he make her understand that he had no intention of fencing with her, without emphasizing the inappropriateness of the situation and thus annoying her further?

"Are you afraid?" Her voice was low and challenging.

Anger combined with reluctant fascination flickered within him. He licked his lips.

"Hardly—unless you count my fear that I shall hurt you."

"With a fleuret? The blade is very dull, and it is buttoned, in any case." She tugged at the laces that fastened the cap over her head. Men who wore fencing caps at all usually chose half caps that left their lower faces exposed; Lady Sarah's one concession to sense was that she wore an unusual full-face cap. She had to have made it herself.

With a determined yank, she loosened the knot at the side of her throat, pulled the laced side seam of the cap apart, and removed the headgear. Beneath it, her curls were tousled and her face was flushed. "That's better. It's terribly difficult to talk with that thing covering my mouth." She tilted her head to the side and studied him. "For once in your life, Lord William, do not worry about what propriety demands. You are obviously trapped here for the day, given the vile weather. Why not enjoy your confinement?"

He stared at her rosy countenance. Never before had a woman seemed so vibrantly appealing—not even the courtesan George had introduced him to the first summer he came down from Oxford. Many ideas for enjoying his confinement sprang to mind, and very few of them had anything to do with fencing.

"Lady Sarah," he began, his voice sounding rough even in his own ears. Doggedly, he continued. "I came out here to apologize, not to fight you—with words or with foils."

She frowned and dropped her arms to her sides.

"No, it is I who should apologize to you," she said in a rush, as though she had been waiting for such an opening and wanted to speak quickly before the opportunity passed. "My words yesterday regarding your status and inheritance were ill-considered and cruel. Even my jest a moment ago, about you being afraid, was uncalled for. I am sorry." She nibbled at her bottom lip, as though she wished to say more. He waited, but she remained silent.

"I accept your apology, and I deeply regret my insults yesterday as well," he said eventually. "Shall we put yesterday behind us, and move on?"

"You could make it up to me." She crossed the dusty floor and picked up the small sword that Sam had discarded on the hay bale along with his cap. "My father's rheumatism makes it impossible for him to fence anymore. Chadwick no longer plays, either, as he says fencing is far too rough for dandies. As a result, I have no one of greater experience to learn from." She returned to his side and held out the practice weapon.

He was sorely tempted. It was a dull, rainy day, after all. And he would be a liar if he didn't admit to himself that it would be vastly entertaining to watch Lady Sarah go through her paces in that outlandish costume.

"I refused to do you a favor yesterday, so I suppose I have no right to ask you to do one for me," she continued. "But my mind is so agitated that I cannot simply sit in the house and work a sampler. I would be most indebted to you for your trouble and expertise."

"Well," he said slowly, trying to give himself time to think, "I suppose the Cates family is mostly to blame for the agitation of your mind." In an instant, he realized that he was actually considering agreeing to this outlandish plan. What would become of him if word got out in London that he made a practice of fencing in Yorkshire barns with wellborn young women?

Be honest, William. Even something this outlandish can't hold a candle to George's scandal. No one would be likely to even mention this minor indiscretion.

For once in his life, William had to admit that having a scoundrel for an older brother had its advantages. "If it would mean so much to you, I'd be honored," he said, reaching for the weapon. As he put his hand around the hilt of the foil, he accidentally brushed Lady Sarah's fingers, and the odd feeling in his stomach flared into something much more distracting.

His opponent, however, seemed to have noticed nothing untoward. She had already turned from him and crossed toward the open area in the center of the barn. "Sam, will you stay by to act as judge?"

"Certainly, if you wish," said the lad, settling onto the hay bale. He picked up the cap next to him and tossed it to William. "Sorry, m'lord. 'Tis quite damp. But 'tis the only cap we've left."

William caught the leather mask and immediately lobbed it back to Sam. "Thank you, but I prefer to fight unencumbered." He shrugged out of his greatcoat, which Sam immediately stepped forward to take, and handed the groom his hat as well. Then he looped the martingale around his wrist and tested the weight of the foil. It was a well-made weapon, if somewhat old and dull.

"You must not fight bareheaded," Lady Sarah

said as she pulled on her own equipment. "Even though our foils are blunted, there is always the possibility of an accident."

"I'll take my chances." Most men in London fought without much protective gear, and he would be damned if he would look like a fribble in front of this minx.

"But—" she began to protest.

He eyed her with the quelling glance he had practiced in front of the mirror during his early days in the diplomatic service. "Do you want to lose your sparring partner before we have even had the chance to fight?"

Her blue eyes, barely visible through the slit in her mask, were mutinous. "Are you always this obstreperous?"

He gave a bark of laughter. "Yes. Do you always say the first thing that enters your head?"

The crinkles at the edges of her eyes indicated that she was smiling. "Unfortunately, yes. Surely you learned that yesterday."

Her self-deprecation was disarming. "We agreed to put that behind us. Shall we proceed?" He moved into position opposite her and raised his foil in salute.

She did likewise. "En garde."

She had certainly mastered the etiquette of the game, he thought as they began.

Within minutes, he realized that she had mastered much more than that. His initial inclination had been to let her score a few easy hits and call it a game. But her initial thrusts were skillful and daring, more than the equal of some of his partners' at Angelo's. She was no master, but she could hold her own.

He quickly changed tacks. It would be as rude as his comments yesterday to play meekly with her just because she was female. She had issued the challenge and was obviously up to the task. The least he could do was give her a fair fight.

He deftly parried a thrust, then executed a fleche that lightly clipped her left side. A sharp gasp of surprise escaped her as she moved quickly to the right. She feinted with a degree of skill that would likely have fooled Sam, but William had already discerned that she regularly used a false the moment she was put on the defensive. He parried it without difficulty, but she instantly fought back and soon caught him squarely on the shoulder.

Even though a leather flower blunted the tip of her foil, the force of the blow was enough to give him pause. It was well they were not fighting with real weapons.

"Touché, Lady Sarah." He nodded at her and stepped back. Moments later, he had her on the defensive again.

At least he's stopped holding back, Sarah thought as she sucked in a deep breath and tried to ascertain her opponent's weakness. That's what Angelo's book had advised. She knew Sam's weaknesses better than her own, which was why she had such luck against him. But Lord William was an unknown quantity, and that made the contest interesting.

She was grateful he had finally agreed to fence with her. It was foolish pride, she knew, but she hoped their encounter would show him that she wasn't just another simpering female, waiting for some gentleman to rescue her. Even if that was, in essence, exactly what she was.

That thought spurred her to parry his latest thrust with somewhat greater force than was necessary. He raised his eyebrows in surprise and counterparried her riposte. The blades clattered together as she bobbed to the left, looking for an opening.

"Good show, Lady Sarah!" Sam cried from the hay bale.

She smiled as she danced further to her left. Lord William stepped back, and she was certain she had him. She moved forward for the final thrust, only to find his blade once again in her way.

Drops of perspiration rolled into her eyes as she continued to move and her breath came in increasingly short gasps.

For such a bookish-looking man, he was a surprisingly good fencer. Not that he looked particularly scholarly at the moment, as he raked his left hand through his increasingly tangled hair. Sarah suspected that the proper Lord William rarely allowed himself to be seen in such a disheveled state. It took much more concentration to keep her mind on strategy when fencing with him than when fencing with Sam.

He attacked with a move she remembered reading about but had never seen executed. Before she could remember the best defense against it, the tip of his fleuret had grazed her stomach.

She felt her cheeks grow hot. Thank heavens for the mask. It was ridiculous to be blushing. It wasn't as though he had touched her himself. It felt almost as if he had, though. Perhaps he had been right, and this had been an unwise idea.

"Touché," she said as they both paused for breath.

"You're not making this easy," he replied, shrugging out of his jacket and handing it to Sam. His fine lawn shirt clung damply to his shoulders and chest, revealing much more of what lay beneath than was strictly proper.

He had been right, after all. This had been a very foolish idea.

"Five more minutes, and then shall we stop?" she asked in a too-bright voice. She sounded like a child caught stealing biscuits from Cook, she thought with disgust.

"As you wish," he said, moving back into position. "There is a watch in my pocket, Sam. Would you be so kind as to keep the time?"

Sarah barely noticed Sam nod and extract the glittering watch. Her eyes were fastened on her opponent. Suddenly, she dearly needed to show him that she could offer him a good fight. They both knew she was a desperate woman in desperate circumstances. But in this one small area, at least, she could prove that she was not completely an object of pity.

They saluted each other once more, then Sarah made a quick opening thrust. Lord William parried it easily. Moments later, he riposted, and she counterattacked and scored a surprise touché on his left shoulder. He grinned, and she forgot all about her small victory. Obviously, he noticed her momentary distraction, as within seconds he had scored a touché on her right side.

The final few minutes passed in a blur. Each of

them enjoyed some degree of success, although Lord William was clearly the superior fencer. Their blades clinked as they maneuvered around the barn, feet moving as quickly as the dusty floor would allow.

"Time!" Sam called, and it was all Sarah could do to refrain from slumping with relief against the nearest wall.

Lord William gave her a final salute, and in his eyes she saw a faint hint of admiration. "Well done, Lady Sarah. You are a worthy adversary."

"Not the equal of your opponents at Angelo's, I'll warrant." She reached for the laces holding her mask in place.

"True enough, although there are several men there I suspect you could best in the right conditions. And you're certainly the finest female opponent I have ever faced."

She pulled off the cap and raised her eyebrows. "You have faced others?"

He shook his head as he retrieved his jacket from Sam. "Hardly. I was giving you a sweeping compliment. The least you could do is be gracious enough to accept it." He laughed without rancor.

She heard herself laugh in return. Heavens, it felt lovely to laugh. She'd done it seldom enough in the last two years, ever since the day her father had admitted the true extent of the family's debts.

"My apologies, sir. Thank you for your kind words. And may I compliment you as well? You are without doubt the most skillful opponent of either sex it has been my pleasure to encounter."

He pulled on his jacket and straightened it across his wide shoulders. "Thank you." He glanced at her. "It is just as well you wear that cap. It would be far too distracting to fence with you if I could see your face."

Unsure exactly what he meant by that comment, she changed the subject. "Luncheon should be ready shortly." She turned toward the doorway, suddenly awkward in his company. "I shall see you in the dining room." Without a backward glance, she pulled an old cloak over her shoulders and dashed into the main section of the barn. Lord William would likely see her abrupt departure as odd, but that mattered not. It was certain that he already thought her peculiar.

Why did she even care what he thought? she wondered as she scurried through the barn. She had much more urgent concerns on her mind. The debt, her reputation, how on earth she was to find another likely husband in a month or two.

It was a shame, really, that Lord William wasn't rich.

Dismissing the thoughts that were forming in her mind, Sarah yanked open the side door to the barn. Pulling the cloak more tightly about her head, she dashed out into the teeming rain.

FOUR

"The sky appears to be clearing at last, Lord William." Sarah let the drawing room curtain fall back into place. The rain had stopped, and a bright moon peeked out occasionally from behind scudding clouds. "You will be able to continue your journey tomorrow, should you wish."

They had spent a pleasant afternoon and evening with her family, playing cards for pennies and reading bits of the day's correspondence aloud to each other. She supposed it had been rather tame entertainment for him, but he had been charming to all. Much more charming than his boisterous brother had been during his visit, truth to tell.

"Kind as your welcome has been, I really must return to London." Their guest stood. "And since the weather is cooperating, I suppose I should repair to my room and prepare. It is a long journey, and it would be best to make an early start."

"Of course." Sarah tried to quell a spurt of disappointment at the thought that he would be leaving so soon. It was ridiculous, she told herself. She could no more pursue a *tendre* for Lord William than she could take fencing lessons at Angelo's. Not only did he not have the blunt her family so desperately needed, he was also far too stuffy for her liking.

She suppressed the image of him grinning as they had fenced in the barn that morning. Well, perhaps *stuffy* was the wrong word. *Proper* was more what she had in mind. And the Harrisons were the last sort of family a proper man would wish to ally himself with.

Sarah loved her family dearly and would not change them if she could. After all, it wasn't as though she was a paragon of normalcy herself. But even she had to admit that an absent-minded father, a mother trapped in 1780, a sister who rarely spoke to humans, and a brother with a penchant for rainbow-hued pantaloons did not exactly raise her status among potential suitors.

And finding a willing suitor was becoming a more pressing necessity as time passed. This afternoon, she had managed to corner her father in his study and extract the details of his meeting with his man of business. Fortunately, no papers had been signed committing them to any payments they could not meet. Her father had quickly dispatched a letter to Ripon instructing his man to cease contacting their creditors, now that the settlement from Lord Cambermere would not be forthcoming. But the situation was grave.

"I don't want to lay the burden of my foolishness on you, child. If I had only managed things better, spent less money on my projects, been less indulgent of your mother's whims, we would not be in such a dilemma," her father had said, his eyes so sad she wanted to weep.

"Do not blame yourself, Father. Was it your fault

the crops failed twice? Or that Grandfather made such ill-advised investments all those years ago?"

He had shaken his head. "I know you are right, but I cannot help but feel responsible."

"I want to help, if I can." She had smiled, hoping to encourage him. "And to help, I must know all the facts."

Eventually, he had told her that Mr. Baines, their man of business, had received a number of new requests for payment, some from creditors her father barely remembered. They had waited a long time, obviously hesitant to press a case against the highest-ranking gentleman in the neighborhood. The fact that they had come forward now had to mean that word was getting out about the family's financial straits.

"And there is no more unentailed land?"

"None. The north pasture was the last of it, and we sold that two summers ago." Her father had smiled brightly. "At least the house will stay in the family."

Cold comfort that was. Yes, the house was entailed and so could not be sold. But the money it could earn in rent was their last defense against their creditors. If the family did not come into some money quickly, they would be forced to let their home to strangers. Sarah had closed her eyes against the thought.

"Thank you for your company this evening," she said now to Lord William, as she accompanied him to the drawing room door. She had had a plan brewing in her mind ever since her meeting with her father, but until this moment she hadn't been certain she had the nerve to carry it out. Realizing that Lord William was leaving the next morning had stiffened her spine. It was now or never. But if she was to manage it at all, she could not bear to have an audience.

As he opened the door, she murmured, "May I have a word with you in private before you retire?"

He raised his eyebrows. "Of course. I shall await you in the foyer." He turned to the assembled company. "Good evening, and my thanks again for your hospitality."

"The pleasure was ours, Lord William," Sarah's father said warmly.

"Have a good journey to London," her mother added.

Sarah watched him go and closed the door behind him. Several minutes later, when Hester was absorbed in a book and her brother and parents had begun a new game of commerce, she quietly rose from her chair and slipped out the door. If anyone noticed her go, they would think she had simply decided to retire early.

He was leaning against the banister, and he smiled as she approached. He should smile more often, she thought. It made him far less intimidating. At the minute, she appreciated anything that made him less intimidating.

"Thank you for waiting."

"I was curious. I thought perhaps you planned to challenge me to a boxing match, since we covered fencing this morning." His grin widened, taking any sting out of his words, and her heart gave an odd little thud.

"Boxing? Far too sedate. I was going to suggest steeplechasing, but the ground is still too damp."

She felt her smile fade. "In all seriousness, though, I do have a favor to ask."

"Please do. I shall be happy to help, if I can. I still feel I have not made proper restitution for my brother's idiocy."

She waved his words away. "You offered for me— I would say that is more than enough." He looked as though he was about to speak, so she held up a hand. "Please let me continue, or I shan't get through this."

He nodded.

"If it would not be too much trouble, I would like you to take me to London with you," she said on a rush of breath.

He blinked. "To London? Tomorrow?"

"It will all be very proper," she hastened to add. "If you agree, I shall ask my mother to accompany us and serve as chaperone."

"Of course, I would be happy to help you," he said. "But this seems very sudden, and the weather is still unpleasant. Wouldn't you prefer to wait a few more weeks, until spring is well and truly sprung, and then take the mail coach? That would give you more time to prepare."

She took a deep breath. This was so humiliating. "I am afraid we cannot take the mail coach. I know my father would provide the money if I asked, but I am afraid that would leave him short of ready funds. I have saved enough by selling eggs and vegetables from our garden to pay for a few nights' lodging along the way, I believe, but I do not think my few shillings will extend to cover the mail coach as well."

He pushed himself away from the pillar and moved closer to her, his eyes alight with excitement. "If it is only a matter of paying for the coach, it would be my pleasure to provide the money you need. It is the least—"

Tears prickled the back of Sarah's eyes at his kindness. Good heavens, when had she become such a watering pot? Missishness wasn't one of her usual failings.

"Thank you, but it isn't simply a matter of money," she interjected. Lowering her voice, she explained. "I love my mother to distraction, but she is notoriously difficult to spur to action. If I were to suggest a trip to London with no fixed date of departure, she would spend months preparing and packing. It would be fall, I'm afraid, before she was ready to depart. But if the choice was between going with you or not going at all, I think she would be more willing to leave quickly."

"Would your father, then, not be a better choice of traveling companion?"

Sarah shook her head. "He will not leave Larkwood for an extended period while our finances are so precarious. He spends much of his time these days providing small payments to various creditors in an effort to keep the wolf from the door."

Lord William smiled. "And you can't exactly prevail upon Hester or Chadwick to accompany you."

Despite herself, Sarah grinned. "I believe that would be a case of the blind leading the blind."

Lord William moved away from her. "But why London? Why now? Is it just that you want an escape from your worries for a little while? I can understand that, certainly. But there are less dramatic ways to do that. Perhaps a visit to York—"

Good heavens, he was going to make her spell it out. "London is becoming busy now, is it not?"

"Yes, the Season is just beginning. Are you eager to see it again?"

"No." She knew it was foolish, but she was too proud to admit that she had never seen the capital. "My father has not gone to London for many years, as he has little interest in political affairs." In the last few years, he had also not had the funds to lease a house in town, she thought but did not add. Their unentailed town house had been sold long ago, when Sarah was an infant.

"Is that what draws you there now—a pressing fascination with Parliament?" He smiled.

Sarah shook her head. "No." She looked away for a moment, feeling ill at what she was about to say. It was not as though Lord William was not cognizant of her financial situation—she had made it clear enough during their meeting the previous evening. But it still felt shameful to state it baldly. "Now that Lord Cambermere has cried off, I must find another husband with deep pockets. It seems to me that the best hunting grounds will be found in London during the Season."

He nodded. "You are right, of course. Every young buck in Britain hoping to settle down makes at least one trip through the marriage mart in spring. Surely one of them would . . . suit your purposes."

She flinched at the note of disgust she heard in his voice. She couldn't blame him, really. She was rather disgusted with herself. But she could do far worse than fish for a fortune if it would save her family.

"I would be happy to pay you back for your trouble, if I am, well, successful." She stared at the floor, unwilling to meet his eyes.

As he watched her, a riot of responses raced through William's mind. He had to admire her grit. Few women in her situation would be willing to abase themselves to such an extent as to beg for something as simple as transportation to London. Certainly, neither her brother nor her sister seemed to be willing to take on the burden of the family disaster. To be truthful, though, Chadwick was too young to be much help, and what little William had seen of Hester seemed to indicate that she was too fey and unworldly for the task.

Even Lord and Lady Glenmont were closing their eyes to disaster. They spoke in vague terms of renovations they planned to do to the house and social events they hoped to hold "when times are better." Lady Glenmont seemed unperturbed during these discussions, although her husband's eyes were haunted. It was clear that neither of them was dealing honestly with their situation.

No, it appeared that Lady Sarah was the only member of the Harrison family who had her feet planted firmly on the ground and her mind focused on reality. He sighed. How well he knew what it was like to be the only levelheaded member of one's family.

And yet, there had to be some other solution than this course of naked fortune hunting she seemed determined to pursue. Most wellborn people thought about money when marrying, of course. But to think of it to the exclusion of all other considerations seemed, well, unseemly.

He couldn't decide whether he was impressed or revolted by her behavior. That was unlike him. In his line of work, he had become used to sizing up people quickly. Not to know how he felt about someone felt deucedly odd.

One thing he did know, however: the Cates family still owed the Harrisons for George's inexcusable behavior. No matter how he felt about Lady Sarah's methods, it was incumbent on him to help her follow whatever course she had decided to pursue. It wasn't as though she had announced that she planned to embark on a life of crime.

Briefly, an image of her dancing about the floor of the barn, brandishing her foil, entered his mind. If she ever decided to forego foils for pistols, she might well have a successful career as a highwayman. Or highwaywoman.

She cleared her throat, and he realized he had been woolgathering.

"There will be no need to repay me for riding in my coach, Lady Sarah," he said briskly, rubbing his hands together. "I would be pleased to provide transportation to London for you and Lady Glenmont, and to pay for your accommodations on the journey as well."

"Truly, I have some money—"

He held up a hand. "Pride is a virtue, Lady Sarah, but taken to extremes it can become a handicap. Let me help you. You may need your funds when you arrive in London." A thought struck him. "Where do you plan to stay when you arrive in the capital? I would offer to accommodate you, but my rooms in St. James's—"

To his surprise, she laughed. "I would not think of

so inconveniencing you. My cousin, Mrs. Templeton, has a small house in London. Each year, she invites us to visit, but we have never accepted her hospitality. I shall write her a letter tonight and ask if we may finally come to stay this year. With luck, the letter will reach the city before we do."

That was one relief, William thought. "Where in the city does your cousin live?"

"I'm not certain. I believe the neighborhood is called Chelsea. I do remember the name of the street—Paradise Row. Doesn't that sound lovely?"

A thought struck him. "Have you ever been to London, Lady Sarah?"

She looked away and sighed. She waited so long to respond that he thought she would ignore his question entirely, but then she shook her head. "No. I have never ventured further from home than Leeds. Truth to tell, I prefer my own fireside. Unlike my brother—who wants to visit America, of all places— I have little desire to see much of the world beyond Yorkshire. I doubt I would ever go to London if the situation didn't require it."

"That is no sin," he replied in a gentle voice, even as he thanked heaven that she had not accepted his offer. A woman who had no interest in the wider world would be miserable married to a diplomat, and said diplomat would likely be miserable married to her.

A small silence fell between them. Then Lady Sarah piped up. "I believe we have reached an agreement, then, Lord William?"

"We have." He placed his hand on the banister. "Take all the time you need to make your preparations. Even if I don't leave until the day after tomorrow, that will be fine." He suppressed a spurt of annoyance at the thought. Tasks and news were no doubt awaiting him in London. The foreign office would still be in turmoil, and he was eager to be back in the midst of it.

His impatience must have shown on his face despite his best efforts, for Lady Sarah replied quickly, "Oh no, we will be ready at first light. You are very kind to take us at all. The last thing I want to do is delay your journey." She smiled. "I cannot thank you enough for your kindness, Lord William. You are doing my family a very great service."

"'Tis nothing." He felt a flush of embarrassment at her effusive appreciation. "I am heading to London anyway. It is a long journey to make alone, and I will appreciate the company." As he said the words, he realized they were true. He suspected that Lady Sarah would make a charming traveling companion. She didn't seem the type to complain about the length of the journey or the condition of the roads. The mother was another matter—just finding room to accommodate her voluminous skirts could be a problem. But he was sure they would all rub along quite well, once they were on the road.

He turned toward the stairs. "Good luck with your travel preparations, Lady Sarah."

"And you as well," she added before turning back to the drawing room to share the news of her impending trip with her family.

As he climbed the stairs, he pondered why he was so anxious to help Lady Sarah. As she had pointed out, he had done what duty required by offering for her. And certainly, she had a charming face and figure, although the realities that came with them—her fortune hunting, her odd hobbies, her even odder family—detracted from that attraction most substantially.

So what was it about her? William smiled to himself. It was obvious that he found her attractive. It was the oldest story in the world. But she desperately wanted a husband, and he didn't want a wife. By all rights, they should have parted company this evening and never seen each other again.

And yet, he couldn't just leave her here to slowly slide into financial ruin. Yes, if George had never crossed their paths the Harrisons would have slid there just as quickly. But George *had* blazed his usual trail of destruction through their lives, and now William couldn't shake a nagging sense of responsibility.

That sense of responsibility had dogged him his whole life, he thought as he reached the top of the stairs and turned left along the corridor to his room. There were days he wished he could be as carefree as George, but a sheepdog might as well wish to become a hunting spaniel.

He opened the door and stepped into the chilly room. A small fire burned in the grate, but it did little to heat the largely empty chamber. Lord, it would be good to be back in London, in so many ways.

Shrugging out of his jacket, he crossed the door to summon Stinson. It would be well to finish his travel preparations early. He wanted to get a good night's rest. He suspected that tomorrow, and the days that followed, were going to require a great deal of energy and good cheer.

FIVE

The landau swayed gently from side to side. It was a lovely carriage, and much more elaborate than the curricle her family had been forced to give up several years ago, when they sold the team. But despite its grandeur, Sarah felt trapped and anxious. They had been traveling for four days, and there were still two days to go—"three or four, if the weather worsens," Lord William had informed them.

Why on earth would people travel for amusement? Sarah asked herself as she shifted in her seat again, trying to get comfortable.

Since her mother's skirts were so enormous, Sarah and Lord William had conceded the entire forward-facing bench to her. It was just as well, as Lady Glenmont had displayed a prodigious ability to sleep in transit. No matter what the route or condition of the road, within ten minutes of their entry into the carriage, her mother would be fast asleep, her jaw sometimes dangling open at a most unladylike angle. Often, she would snuggle up against the side of the carriage, and Sarah was relieved that Lord William had offered to sit on the opposite bench. It would have been embarrassing, really, to have her mother curl up on the gentleman's shoulder as she slumbered.

But with her mother occupying one of the two benches, it was unavoidable that Sarah and Lord William would spend the entire journey side by side on the opposite seat. Normally, this would have been no hardship, as the carriage was spacious. And it wasn't that Lord William was overly tall—in fact, he was only a few inches taller than Sarah herself. But despite that, she felt oddly crowded as she sat next to him on the bench. She did her best to prevent even her skirts from brushing against his boots. But the more she tried, the more difficult it seemed to become to avoid any contact.

But contact was something to be avoided at all costs, she had learned, to her embarrassment. Once, when her hand had rested in their host's as she descended from the carriage, her cheeks had flamed like a schoolgirl's. And when he had held her elbow, in a perfectly gentlemanly manner, to guide her through the crowded foyer of an inn the previous evening, her heart had slammed against her chest like a blacksmith's hammer on an anvil. At the moment, she was all too aware that his shoulder rested just inches from her own. From the day they had fenced in the barn, she remembered how broad his shoulders were—uncommonly wide for such a slight man.

Really, she was behaving like a moonstruck schoolgirl. It had to stop.

"Do you enjoy travel, Lord William?" she asked now, partly to break the disturbing train of her thoughts and partly because she was truly interested. During the course of their journey, he had talked fondly of the years he had spent in the diplomatic service. She learned he had been to most of Europe's major capitals, with the exception of Paris. It sounded like a terribly disruptive sort of life to her, but she supposed her quiet life in Yorkshire would seem terribly dull to him.

"I do, actually." He leaned back against the squabs and she reflexively shifted her weight toward the other side of the carriage. "If I spend too long in any one place, I get restless. And every place I go has so many intriguing aspects: new sights, new foods, new customs."

"But is it not difficult, going to lands where you don't speak the language?"

He crossed one foot over the opposite knee. "It can be, yes. Fortunately, I am fluent in German and French and have a fairly good command of Latin. With those languages, I find I am able to make myself understood in most parts of the Continent. Even in Russia, French is widely spoken and understood among the diplomatic corps."

"How did you come to learn so many languages?"

He brushed at his sleeve, apparently having spied some tiny bit of lint that was invisible to her. "I grew up speaking both English and German at home, as my mother was German. She came to England as a junior lady-in-waiting to Queen Charlotte. A tutor of mine had a particular fondness for French, and so I learned it at a much younger age than many boys and picked it up quite quickly. The Latin was part of the curriculum at school." He smiled. "Once you know one foreign language, it becomes easier to learn another. Soon, it is like eating sweets—you cannot stop yourself."

She laughed. "My mother insisted we all try to learn French, but only Hester appeared to have any facility for it. I'm afraid that, despite Mother's best efforts, the main words I know in French all have to do with fencing."

"That may put you at a decided disadvantage in London's ballrooms, unless you take it into your head to challenge one of your rivals to a duel." His voice had a very slight mocking edge, but she decided to ignore it. Lord William had been most pleasant to her during the journey. She had no desire to pick a fight with him.

"I suppose if I find myself in the midst of any disputes, it will be better to fight with words than with foils." She let out an exaggerated sigh. "I suppose I shall have to get used to your strange southern customs."

He laughed. "I suppose you shall. I will just have to teach you to distinguish your *on-dits* from your *bon mots*."

She tried to translate in her head using what little French she had managed to retain. "My 'someone says' from my 'good words'?" she asked, puzzled.

"Close. An *on-dit* is a bit of gossip, while a *bon mot* is a witty saying."

"I shall try to remember that." She shook her head as she realized, not for the first time, that she was taking a journey that involved much more than miles traveled by carriage. In undertaking this desperate jaunt to London, she was leaping from a world she knew to one that was likely to be as strange to her as the Louisiana Territory.

"If you find yourself in any difficulties while you

are in London, Lady Sarah, please do not hesitate to send word to me. I am at your service, at least as long as I am in the city." He looked her square in the eyes, and his voice was earnest.

"You are very kind, Lord William, but you have done so much for us already." Despite her entreaties, he had insisted on paying for their lodgings along the road. The first evening, their disagreement had threatened to attract attention in the front room of the inn, with Sarah insisting that she could pay her share and Lord William insisting that he wouldn't hear of it. Surprisingly, Sarah's mother had put an end to the argument by taking Lord William's side.

"Really, Sally, you are too headstrong," she had admonished her daughter. "You are distressing Lord William."

With both of them arrayed against her, she had had no choice but to give in. It would be useful to have a small nest egg to rely on in London, she had to admit, even though it galled her to lean on Lord Cambermere's brother for anything. All it did was cement the ridiculous notion he had that he was somehow responsible for her.

"As you wish, Lady Sarah," he said now in a stiff voice, in response to her refusal of his assistance.

"Oh dear, Lord William, I am afraid I have offended you again." Botheration! She seemed to have a talent for insulting the man. Either he was very easily put out, or she had spent so much time in the company of her family that what few social skills she had ever possessed had deserted her.

"I am not offended," he said, his tone belying his words. "And my offer stands. If there is anything you need in London, be assured that I will be happy to help. I still think I should write to George and ask him—"

"No." They had discussed this in great detail yesterday. Lord William wanted to bully his brother into providing the settlement George had verbally promised Sarah at their betrothal. And while it was indeed true that, morally, the duke should pay, the thought of asking Lord William to beg for her mortified her. Even if he did succeed, she would always then feel beholden to his family, as though she had purloined their money under false pretenses. She knew she was being ridiculous, but she could not help how she felt. She would find the money her family needed some other way.

Lord William subsided against the side of the carriage with a gusty sigh. "Has anyone ever told you, Lady Sarah, that you are uncommonly stubborn?"

"Yes, but I refused to believe them." To her relief, he smiled at her small joke, and the discussion turned into more pleasant channels. When he wasn't attempting to give her assistance she didn't want, Sarah thought, Lord William was a very pleasant traveling companion. He was well read and well informed, yet he didn't try to dominate the conversation as so many men did. And even though he raised his eyebrows over a few of her stories—such as her tale of the time she and Chadwick almost fell from the barn roof when they were children—he had the sense not to comment on her lack of propriety. It was none of his business, anyway. When they reached the capital, they would go their separate ways. He would return to the diplomatic affairs he obviously relished, and she would begin looking in earnest for a wealthy husband.

That thought reminded her of something. "There is one way you can help me right now, Lord William."

"With pleasure." His smile made him look truly eager.

"My cousin Mrs. Templeton—the lady with whom we will be staying—once mentioned that there are gentlemen in Town during the Season who are better known for their purses than for their bloodlines."

He nodded. "More and more of them every year. There are great fortunes being made in all sorts of new ventures, from cotton mills to canals. And the men who are amassing them often come from humble backgrounds. There is also a growing number of wealthy men who own shops."

"Would such men be likely to frequent a place such as Almack's?" She hesitated as his face clouded. "That is the name of the establishment where everyone goes to dance, is it not?"

"It is, although the Almack's definition of 'everyone' is rather select. I doubt any of the rich Cits you have in mind could cross the threshold under the patronesses' gimlet eyes." He steepled his fingers in front of his face as he considered the issue. "If you should like to meet them, I would suggest a visit to the theater, or perhaps Astley's circus."

She grinned. "Those sound much more to my taste, in any case. Even my governesses were forced to admit that I have little skill as a dancer."

"That surprises me," he said, his voice low. "When

we were fencing, I thought you uncommonly grace-ful."

She felt her eyes widen. It was one of the only genuine compliments he had paid her during the brief period of their acquaintance, and she was so taken aback she did not know where to look. She felt a slow, unfamiliar flush creeping up her cheeks. Even her ears were aflame. How preposterous.

"Thank you, Lord William. Fencing is something I understand. But when it comes to remembering which foot goes where and whose hand I should take during a quadrille, I am at sea. I don't get much practice," she added hastily, in case he viewed her lack of skill as yet another cause to pity her. "And, truly, I've never felt much interest in dancing. I think the theater would be much more to my taste."

"What sort of theater do you like?"

Heavens. She had walked right into another conversational swamp. She had read about the theater, of course, and her parents had talked about visiting the theaters of London in their youth, but she had never been to one. On her brief excursion to Leeds all those years ago, she had spent most of her time visiting relatives and exploring the shops. But how could she admit that, as well as knowing little of French or dancing, she was an ignoramus in the theater as well?

"Shakespeare!" she exclaimed, a trifle too loudly. There, that could not be wrong. She had at least read the plays, in a worn old volume her father had inherited. She could hold her own in this conversation.

"One of my favorites," her companion replied,

and she felt the tension in the back of her neck ebb away. To her relief, the conversation moved into a discussion of the merits of various Shakespearean heroes.

It was exhausting, she thought, this business of ensuring that she gave Lord William no cause to think she needed assistance. Once they arrived in London and bid each other farewell she would feel much easier. Neither her mother nor her cousin would interfere with or criticize her plans to any great degree, she felt certain. She could be back to relying on herself alone, and that would be a relief. Relying on others led only to heartbreak, as she had learned all too well from her brief association with the Duke of Cambermere.

It was almost dusk that evening when the carriage rolled to a stop in the courtyard of a small inn in an anonymous village.

"I shall go to find out whether any rooms are available," Lord William said as John Coachman opened the carriage door and lowered the steps. Rising without any apparent sign of the stiffness Sarah felt in every bone of her body, he levered himself through the doorway and leaped lightly to the ground. Despite her best intentions, she found herself watching him as he strolled through the waning daylight toward the doorway of the inn.

"He cuts a fine figure," her mother said from the other side of the carriage, making Sarah jump. She had not realized her parent had awakened. Lady Glenmont had spent almost the entire afternoon asleep.

"Yes," Sarah replied. "He has gone to see about securing us rooms for the night. It appears that we are roughly halfway through our journey, and I for one am glad." She hoped to distract her mother from any discussion of Lord William's figure, fine or otherwise.

But Lady Glenmont was not to be dissuaded. "A much more handsome gentleman than his brother. Too bad 'tis the duke who holds the purse strings in the family. Otherwise, you might have happily accepted the offer from this one."

Happily? Could she have been happy married to Lord William? Sarah pondered the question she had been considering intermittently ever since their journey to London had begun. Every time her mind had wandered down that path, however, she had called a firm halt to her daydreams.

"Perhaps," said Sarah, looking toward the door of the inn. "Lord William tells me that this inn is renowned for its food, particularly its excellent lamb."

Her mother brightened up at this news. "With mint jelly? I do so love lamb with mint jelly, and it has been ever so long since we have had it at home."

Sarah breathed a sigh of relief as she turned her mother's thoughts to less contentious matters. Within a few minutes, Lord William had emerged from the inn.

"We are in luck. Two good rooms are available— I checked them myself." He extended his hand toward Sarah's mother. "Lady Glenmont, may I assist you?"

"Thank you," the countess said, grabbing Lord

William's hand as she angled herself sideways so that her panniers would precede her through the narrow carriage door. Obviously, Lord Cambermere's carriage had been manufactured long after wide skirts had gone out of fashion. Every evening, it was a bit of an engineering feat to extricate Lady Glenmont from the vehicle.

Sarah glanced outside to see several people in the courtyard observing her mother curiously. Let them stare, she thought. If they had been through some of the things Lady Glenmont had endured, perhaps they would take refuge in fantasy and play-acting, too.

With a prodigious rustle, the countess popped through the doorway and made her awkward way down the steps. From the look on Lord William's face, he was supporting most of her weight with his hand as she toddled to the ground. He said not a word, however, and just smiled as she righted herself.

"Thank you," the countess said as she moved away from the carriage so that her daughter could alight.

"Lady Sarah?" Lord William said, extending his hand.

This was the part of the journey that Sarah had come to both anticipate and dread. But there was no help for it—she could not, in all politeness, refuse his assistance. She placed her gloved hand in his.

The spark of awareness that had quickly become a familiar companion shot through her fingers. As she knew it would, the skin on the back of her neck began to prickle, and her breath caught in the back of her throat. This was ridiculous. Certainly, she was not a highly social person, but was she so sequestered that the mere touch of a man's hand could send her into a panic?

She fairly ran down the steps toward the cobblestones. "Thank you, my lord," she said as her feet touched solid ground again. She withdrew her hand and tucked it under her opposite elbow, and he frowned.

Had she been too obvious in her haste? Good heavens, she would have to be more careful. She did not want him to think she disliked him, after all he had done for her family.

Half an hour later, after freshening up in a plain but clean chamber below the eaves, Sarah and her mother sat in a small private room off the taproom, awaiting the arrival of Lord William.

"I wonder what can be keeping him?" Lady Glenmont asked.

"I suspect he is completing some letters," Sarah replied. She knew from their conversations in the carriage that he maintained a voluminous correspondence with friends and relations across the British Isles and abroad. In addition, he had mentioned the excitement that was afoot at the foreign office due to the recent abdication of Napoleon, and that he wanted to ensure that he would be considered for any postings arising from the news.

"It's high time I was abroad again," he had said.

He was more than welcome to his wanderings, Sarah thought, rubbing a sore spot on her shin where she had banged it against the carriage seat earlier in the day. Once this trip to London was done, she heartily hoped that she would be able to retire to the country once more, where things were familiar and one didn't spend hours on end trapped in close quarters.

"Good evening, ladies. I trust your room was to your satisfaction?"

She looked up as Lord William entered the room and settled gracefully into a wooden chair on the opposite side of the small dining table. No sooner had he adjusted his coat and straightened his neck-cloth than the innkeeper bustled in with a pitcher of ale.

"M'lord, good evening," the slight gray-haired man said with a small bow. "Is there anything in particular I can fetch you while you are awaiting your meal?"

Lord William eyed the pitcher with interest. "You have seen to slaking my thirst, which is my most pressing concern at the moment, thank you. All else can wait, unless the ladies would like something?"

Sarah shook her head. "We are well served, thank you."

With another small bow, the innkeeper set a sturdy glass on the table, filled it with ale, and departed. As he left, Lord William shot Sarah a sheepish grin.

"It's rather splendid, actually, traveling the countryside in George's coach. Even though the innkeepers know I am not the duke, the carriage alone seems to spur everyone to provide excellent service. I am never so popular when I arrive on horseback, with no crests or gold leaf to impress anyone."

It was impossible to tell whether that fact an-

AN HONORABLE MATCH 89

noyed him or not. Sarah rather thought it didn't. From what she had learned of the man in their short acquaintance, it seemed clear that he had little interest in the trappings of his position.

He leaned back in his chair and sipped his ale. "It is good to stop moving at last," he observed. "How are you finding the journey, Lady Glenmont?"

"Perfectly pleasant," her mother replied, smiling at him over the rim of her lemonade glass.

Sarah had not seen her mother as cheerful in many months. It was clear the countess was charmed by the duke's brother. Thinking of the duke brought a question to mind Sarah had meant to ask this afternoon. "Do you expect to have word of your brother waiting for you when you return to London?"

Lord William shrugged. "It is unlikely. Even if he had written en route and sent the letter back on the ship's return journey, it is doubtful whether it would have reached England already. Besides, George is an erratic correspondent at the best of times." He raised his glass to his lips again and drank deeply before continuing. "If I hear any news of him on his travels, it will likely be unpleasant, delivered by some mutual acquaintance interested in keeping me informed of my brother's latest debacle."

"And if there *is* a debacle, what shall you do?" Sarah suspected she already knew the answer to this question.

Their traveling companion gave a theatrical sigh and rolled his eyes toward the ceiling. "I suppose I shall find myself booking a passage to Italy, if I am not already otherwise engaged on foreign office business."

Sarah smiled at a young serving girl, who had just hurried in with a platter of bread, which she set on the table along with a small pot of butter. Sarah picked up the plate and offered it to Lord William. "I'm beginning to suspect it is due to your brother, and not to the foreign office, that you are so well traveled. It must be tiring, running about the world repairing his disasters." She tried to keep her voice light and devoid of any trace of the bitterness she still felt. She herself was, after all, one of the duke's "disasters."

If Lord William noticed a hint of sharpness in her voice, he gave no indication. "What else can I do?" he asked, taking a large slice of bread and putting it on his plate. "One cannot exactly change families. One must do the best with one's birthright."

She felt a pang of sympathy at the underlying tone of frustration in his voice. Well did she know how love and annoyance, loyalty and panic, could be combined in one seething mess where family was concerned.

"True enough," piped up the countess as she buttered her own bread. "I always say to the earl that we are very fortunate in that our children are all well behaved and unexceptional. No offense meant to your brother, Lord William."

"None taken," he said between bites of bread. "I am an ardent admirer of propriety myself, believe me."

Sarah said nothing, as she was afraid that anything she might say would be misinterpreted. She fully understood why Lord William would be so devoted to good behavior—if she had a brother like the duke, she would be the same. But they had already had several conversations in the carriage about the difference between decorum and boredom, and had come to no conclusion that satisfied them both.

"And what is your opinion, Lady Sarah?" he asked, glancing behind him as the serving girl returned with a platter of lamb. As the maid offered the plate to each diner in turn and the fragrant aroma of roasted meat drifted over the table, Sarah felt her stomach rumble. She waited until everyone had selected a portion and the serving girl had departed, before replying to Lord William's question.

"I believe decorum is valuable," she said carefully. She had no urge to stir up a debate. She and Lord William had been getting along so well.

"Even to the extent of the things one does in the privacy of one's own home?"

She sighed. "What one does in private should be less restricted, as long as it does not hurt others. Everyone does things behind closed doors that I am sure they would not wish to see bruited about in public. That does not mean one should not do them."

"Even if they are unseemly?"

"Even so." She set down her cutlery with a clatter. "Lord William, I know my fencing distresses you, but truly, no one is harmed. And it is really none of your affair."

"I think Sally cuts a fine figure fencing," her mother interjected as she reached for the small bowl of mint jelly. "Looks a bit odd, true, but who am I to say who dresses in a peculiar way?" She gave her companions a broad smile before returning her attention to her meal.

Sarah felt a rush of affection. Trust her mother to stand up for her. *We eccentrics have to stick together,* she thought.

"I would not say she looks *odd* while fencing, exactly. Unconventional, certainly, but not odd," Lord William said with an enigmatic light in his eyes.

A funny shiver crept up Sarah's spine. Somehow the direction of the conversation had changed, and its undertones made her uncomfortable.

"More bread?" she asked brightly, proffering the plate to Lord William.

Blessedly, he took a slice, took her hint, and changed the topic.

The weather improved the further south they traveled, and within two more days, their carriage had reached London. The frantic activity of the capital was a revelation to Sarah. Everywhere she looked were horses, carriages, people, shops, houses, and animals. The road was a riot of constant motion and noise, the cries of costermongers mixing with shouts of coach drivers and the clatter of hooves on cobblestones. Despite her overwhelming urge to stare out the side of the carriage like a child observing a fancy dress ball, Sarah forced herself to ignore most of the tumult and converse quietly with Lord William. She didn't want to give him any more reason than he already had to consider her a provincial rustic.

Not that it mattered. Shortly, her curious association with the duke's brother would end. He would return to his books and his diplomatic duties, and she would begin her vital task of finding the fortune that would save her family.

From the corner of her eye, she observed Lord William's profile. In the late afternoon sunlight, his eyes reminded her once again of emeralds. One unruly lock of hair brushed the top of his brows. She would be willing to wager that Lord William would have Stinson trim the offending hair by the end of the evening, in order to present his usual flawless facade to the world by tomorrow morning.

He was a stuffed shirt, to be certain, but she had to admit she would miss his company. On the bright side, at least she would be done fending off his endless attempts to proffer assistance.

"I think we're drawing close to Mary's street," said the countess, craning her neck to get a better view of a storefront they had just passed. "It has been years since I've been here, of course, but I am certain I remember that millinery shop."

"You may well," Lord William replied, reaching for his hat and straightening the brim. "We are in Chelsea now."

Within five minutes, the carriage had made its slow way through the crush of vehicles and drawn up to the pavement before a pretty brick town house. A wrought-iron gate enclosed stairs leading down to a doorway below the street, while another set of steps led up to a bright blue door capped with an arched fanlight.

A moment later, the carriage door opened and John Coachman peered in. "We've arrived at Mrs. Templeton's home, Lady Glenmont," he announced, lowering the steps and extending his hand.

Instead of the joy she had expected to feel on reaching their destination, a wave of sadness washed over Sarah. The journey was over. This was truly good-bye.

"Lord William," she began as her mother started the arduous process of exiting the carriage. "I cannot thank you enough for all you have done for us."

He waved her gratitude aside. "It was nothing, truly. I am in your debt for your company. The trip passed much more quickly than my journey north." He nodded for her to follow the countess, who was now standing on the pavement straightening her skirts. "And I must thank you for your good spirits about this entire affair. You would have been well within your rights to decry my brother's name throughout the length and breadth of England."

"What good would that have done?" she said with a shrug. "It would have only intensified the scandal, and that would not suit my purposes at all. Nor yours, I am sure."

"All the same, you have taken a most levelheaded approach. And remember, if there is ever anything I can do to help you—"

"—I'll be certain to let you know." She smiled, but her tone left neither of them in any doubt that she had no intention of accepting any future assistance from the Cates family.

Sarah picked up her skirts and descended the carriage steps with the assistance of John Coachman, just as the front door of the town house flew open.

"Margaret! Sarah! What a delightful surprise it

was to receive your letter!" A middle-aged woman in a blue silk day dress hurried down the stairs, a stray curl escaping from her gray coiffure as she did so.

Sarah barely remembered her cousin, as it had been eleven years since Mrs. Templeton had visited them at Larkwood Manor. But the warmth of her greeting left no doubt that it was she.

"I am sorry that we have arrived so precipitately," Sarah said as she moved toward their hostess. "I hope that it is not an inconvenient time." As she said it, she wondered just what she would do if Mrs. Templeton could not host them. She had been so occupied with plans for meeting eligible gentlemen in London that she had spared barely a thought for their accommodation.

Mrs. Templeton instantly put her fears at rest. "Not at all! I was just saying to Mr. Templeton last week that I hoped this would be the year that you would finally respond to my entreaties. And here you are!" She had gotten to the bottom step and reached out to hug Sarah's mother. "My, Sarah, how you've changed since the last time we met!"

Sarah smiled. Before her cousin could launch into any descriptions of baby fat, Sarah looked behind her to see Lord William emerging from the carriage, his hat already atop his head. "Mrs. Templeton, may I introduce you to Lord William Cates? He was kind enough to allow us to ride with him on his return journey to London."

Recognition flickered across the older woman's face as she dropped a brief curtsey. Sarah had outlined the bare bones of her predicament in her letter to her cousin, so Mrs. Templeton was well aware of all that had transpired between the Cateses and the Harrisons. "It is a pleasure to meet you, my lord. Will you join us for some refreshment?"

As John Coachman and Stinson unloaded the Harrisons' few traveling cases from the top of the carriage, Lord William shook his head with a rueful smile. "Thank you, Mrs. Templeton, but I'm afraid I must decline. I suspect there are some matters awaiting me at home." He turned his attention to the countess. "So this is farewell, Lady Glenmont. I very much enjoyed traveling with you, and I hope we shall see each other around Town during your stay."

Sarah's mother giggled—actually giggled—and held out her hand, which Lord William took and gallantly kissed. "The pleasure was ours, Lord William. And, indeed, I suspect we shall see each other often around Town."

Not if I can help it, Sarah thought with a twinge of sadness. He would likely be in the company of other noblemen, while she would need to focus her attention on rather less exalted gentlemen.

"I hope we shall," said Lord William before he turned to Sarah.

"And I meant what I said," he murmured in a voice meant for her alone. "Here is my card. I am at your service."

"Really, Lord William, you have more than repaid your brother's debt," she said as she accepted the small bit of paper, realizing she sounded ungracious but eager to absolve him of any lingering sense of responsibility he felt for her.

"I know," he said, his eyes locked on hers. "I'm not making this suggestion out of guilt. I am making it in the spirit of friendship." He reached for her hand and lifted it, then brushed his lips lightly across her knuckles.

Sarah felt as though the pavement had tilted suddenly toward the street.

"Your servant, Lady Sarah," he said in a low voice. And then, before she truly realized what was happening, he was gone.

"He seemed like a nice gentleman," Mrs. Templeton said as several servants hastened across the pavement to collect the traveling cases and begin ferrying them up the stairs. "It is a shame such good manners don't run in the family."

Sarah cast a glance about her, as if every passerby was eavesdropping in the hopes of catching wind of her scandalous jilting. "It is, indeed," she murmured, making for the stairs before her cousin began a full-blown examination of Sarah's shame out here in the street.

To her relief, the two older women followed her. Within moments, they'd reached the relative safety of Mrs. Templeton's foyer. As the door closed behind them, Sarah breathed a deep, silent sigh of relief. The long journey was over, she'd said goodbye to Lord William, and they'd arrived to a warm welcome in London.

Now all that remained was to find a rich, willing husband in a month or two. How difficult could that be?

"You've become quite the celebrity," Mrs. Templeton told Sarah as the butler took their wraps.

"What do you mean?" Sarah asked, even as she knew the question was moot.

"It's been the talk of Town! Not that I would

worry, if I were you," her cousin reassured her as they climbed the stairs. "In a few days, all anyone will remember is your name, and few of the other details."

Just tell me the details, Sarah barely refrained from shouting. Mrs. Templeton was being maddeningly vague, but Sarah could hardly be rude to her.

"What do you mean?" she asked in a strained voice as they reached the top of the stairs and her relative ushered them into a small, pleasant sitting room overlooking Paradise Row.

"Why, the newspapers! Of course, you haven't seen them, having been traveling for so long. Here I am chattering away, and you won't have any idea what I mean. I'm sorry, dear." She bustled over to a table in a corner of the room, where several newspapers sat in an untidy pile, and picked up the journal on the top of the stack. "Here, you can see it for yourself," she said, proffering the paper and pointing to a column in the top right corner of the folded page.

Sarah took it and sank into the nearest chair as she read:

> *The Duke of C——e has left Town for an extended holiday on the Continent with his new duchess. The church register of All Saints, Chelsea, reveals that the new duchess is not the duke's recent intended, Lady Sarah Harrison of Larkwood Manor, Newtonbridge, Yorkshire, eldest daughter of Lord Glenmont, but rather Miss Harriet Partridge, until this very week the toast of Drury Lane.*

Drury Lane. That was why Lord William had thought she might recognize Miss Partridge's name. Good heavens, Lord Cambermere had married an actress! Sarah knew little of the ways of Town, but she knew enough to realize that the duke had likely been very well acquainted with Miss Partridge before his marriage.

Not only had Lord Cambermere jilted her, he had jilted her for his *mistress.*

As Sarah continued to read, her head began to buzz.

> *The newlyweds are planning to spend two months in Italy, which is an ingenious strategy for avoiding the firestorm of innuendo that has already swept through the* haut ton *at this shocking revelation.*

Firestorm. Innuendo. Shocking revelation. Sarah had feared all of these things, and more. She just had not expected them to come to pass so soon.

"Sarah! Are you well? Oh my dear, would you like a cup of tea?" Mrs. Templeton's voice seemed to come from very far away.

Sarah felt herself shake her head. "No, thank you, I will be fine in a moment." The buzzing had intensified. Soon she realized that it wasn't an amorphous hum, but rather a torrent of words rushing through her brain.

Would rich men who did not move in *ton* circles read such reports? More important, would they care? Or would they care only for the fact that her father was an earl, and ignore the fact that her reputation was in tatters?

She looked at the article again. "Lady Sarah Harrison of Larkwood Manor, Newtonbridge, Yorkshire, eldest daughter of Lord Glenmont." There was no chance that anyone in England would mistake her for anyone else. Anger began to build in her as she glanced at the column again. The writer had paid Lord Cambermere the courtesy of partially disguising his name, even though *he* was the guilty party in all this! For her, the victim, there was no such discretion.

It was all so unfair!

Breathe, she reminded herself for probably the hundredth time in the last week. *Don't forget to breathe.*

"You mustn't worry about this, Sarah! Every day, the newspapers move on to something new. This journal is several days old. Everyone has probably forgotten all about it by now." Mrs. Templeton's voice was clearer now, but Sarah still couldn't look at her.

It had been painful enough writing the letters she had carefully penned and mailed from each inn along the way, informing friends and relatives that she would not, in fact, be the next duchess of Cambermere. But at least she had shared the initial news of her betrothal with only a few kind souls, none of whom were likely to be anything but sympathetic.

But this—this! Everyone in England—well, everyone who read the *Morning Post,* at any rate—would now be witness to her humiliation.

"Did any of the other newspapers mention . . . the duke's elopement?" she asked in a small voice as someone pressed a cup of tea into her hand.

Her question was met by silence. Sarah finally looked up to see her embarrassed hostess staring at the stack of newspapers on the corner table.

"All of those?" Sarah whispered.

Mrs. Templeton nodded. "But, dear gel, you really shouldn't take this so much to heart. Truly, I assure you, the scandal will pass in a week or two."

In a daze, Sarah set the teacup on a small table beside her chair and crossed the room to the pile of newspapers. The worst of the gossip would soon evaporate, she thought as she flipped through the journals, but the whiff of impropriety attached to her name would linger for at least the length of the Season. She just had to hope and pray that there was at least one wealthy single gentleman somewhere in London who did not read the *Morning Post.*

Or the *Herald,* she thought as she continued to thumb through the newspapers. Or the *Chronicle,* the *Packet,* or the *Reporter.*

She thought of Lord William, making his way to St. James's, and her heart turned over. For a gentleman whose primary concern in life was propriety, the coming weeks were not going to be pleasant. Not pleasant at all.

SIX

William inhaled deeply and smiled. The spring air was just the tonic he needed after spending all morning in meetings in a dim office deep inside Whitehall.

The meetings had been productive, though. Excitement was running high in the aftermath of Napoleon's dramatic abdication. Castlereagh had convened a large meeting of various members of the foreign service to discuss plans for the upcoming peace conference in Vienna. William had tried, subtly, to let his superiors know that he would welcome the opportunity to participate in the conference. Not only would it be the most important diplomatic event of the last decade, it would also give him the perfect excuse to get away from London for an extended period. The last week had been an excruciating time for anyone connected with George to be in Town. Normally, William had a very thick skin—years of living in his brother's exuberant shadow had toughened him—but even he had found recent days taxing.

"Cates!"

William turned his head toward the voice and suppressed a groan. Striding toward him with a wide grin was David Foxley, Town bon vivant and widely renowned addlepate. William snuck a quick glance at his pocket watch. With luck, Foxley was on his way to White's—he was usually an early arrival at the club, all the better to be in his cups and up to his neck in debt before suppertime. If Foxley was destined for White's, perhaps he wouldn't be inclined to linger long in the middle of Old Bond Street.

"Foxley." William extended his hand to his old school acquaintance and braced himself for the sly comment that was surely coming next.

"Good to see you out and about," the blond man said with a sickly smile. "Thought you might be hunkered down at home, waiting for the storm to pass."

"'Tis none of my affair," William said tightly, repeating the words he had spoken so often they had become as familiar to him as his own name.

"True enough, true enough," Foxley said, slapping him on the back. "Still, you're the one to bear the repercussions, eh? I hear that Cambermere has scarpered for Italy. A fine time I suppose he's having there, eh? He and Harriet are probably living life on a grand scale."

"I suppose they are." William kept his voice bland, even as he envisioned the torrent of letters that were likely to start arriving any day now from his foreign service colleagues in Naples. George's ship had stopped for several days in Portugal en route, and a missive had already arrived from the British consul in Lisbon describing an escapade involving George, Harriet, several bottles of port, and a fountain.

He gave Foxley what he hoped was a carefree smile.

"So what was so dreadful about this woman in Yorkshire that George bolted? Homely, was she?"

An image of Lady Sarah in her fencing garb popped unbidden into William's mind. "Far from it. Lady Sarah shares no blame for this affair."

"As you say," Foxley said in an indulgent voice. "It has the *ton* twittering, I can tell you."

"You don't have to tell me," William muttered, glancing at his watch openly now. "If you'll excuse me, I must be on my way."

"Of course, of course. Give my regards to your sister-in-law when next you see her. Fine woman, that Harriet." Foxley's lip curled into an unpleasant leer as he bowed and took his leave.

William continued along Old Bond Street and kept walking as it turned into New Bond Street. Only a thin veneer of civilization kept him from smashing his fist into the nearest wall as he strode along the pavement.

He had expected the *ton* to be absorbed in the scandal, of course. But he had hoped the affair would not expand to such monumental proportions. The columns in the newspapers had continued for a solid week, beginning the day after William had left London. There had been editorials about the duties of the higher levels of the aristocracy to marry within their class. In the last few days, caricatures by Rowlandson and lesser artists had begun appearing in the windows of print shops throughout the city. The most popular one portrayed George, his vacant face alight with glee, dandling a barely clad Harriet on his knee. The caption read "The Duchess of Drury Lane—A Dramatic Triumph!"

William had already received three of them, anonymously, by post.

Even his superiors in the foreign office, gentlemen not normally given over to gossip, had remarked upon the growing firestorm. "See your brother is in a bit of a fix," Lord Castlereagh had commented with admirable restraint.

William wondered how Lady Sarah was coping with the onslaught. At least he had been dealing with the repercussions of George's follies for his entire adult life. All of this would be new to Lady Sarah.

As soon as he had realized the extent of the disaster, he had returned to the little town house in Paradise Row. In fact, he had attempted to call on Lady Sarah three times. On each visit, the butler had informed him in stiff tones that Lady Sarah was not at home.

She had told him that she wanted no further help from him, and it appeared she intended to stay true to her word. Initially, her determination seemed rooted in stubborn pride. Now, he suspected, it was founded mainly in humiliation.

If he were Lady Sarah, he would not want anything to do with the Cates family either.

It wasn't as though he could really do anything concrete to help her. Normally, he might have been able to introduce her to some marriageable gentlemen of her station, men with enough blunt to help resolve her family's financial crisis. But his social status was almost as low as hers at the minute. And he could not guarantee how most men of his acquaintance would react on being introduced to England's most famous jilt.

He had thought a number of times about sending her some funds to support her visit in London, but he knew she would be too proud to accept them.

Without realizing it, he had walked all the way to Oxford Street. He glanced right, along the busy pavement, and gritted his teeth. There was no help for it. He was almost out of stationery, and the print shop from which he customarily ordered his paper was about a five-minute walk down Oxford Street. No matter how many sneering denizens of the *ton* he encountered, he would not let them keep him from going about his errands in a normal manner. He had done nothing wrong.

Just like Lady Sarah.

He cursed his thoughts under his breath as he stalked down the pavement, nodding but not stopping to speak to several acquaintances. All that he could do for Lady Sarah—all that she would allow him to do for her—he had done. She had made it clear that she wanted to concentrate on her rather grasping but completely understandable hunt for a fortune. His responsibility to her was done.

Why, then, could he not put the minx out of his mind?

He even thought he saw her everywhere. Yesterday, it had been a petite dark-haired woman passing by in a carriage, who on closer inspection was a good decade older than Lady Sarah. A few days before that, he had thought a woman strolling on the Embankment wore a bonnet just like one

Lady Sarah had sported. And now, he thought he spotted her gazing into a milliner's window.

He stopped and squinted at the figure a few shop fronts away. By God, this time it *was* Lady Sarah. None of the other women who had resembled her had quite her determined mien.

She was wearing the same dull-colored pelisse she had worn on the journey to London, along with the bonnet he remembered. Her hands were clasped behind her back.

He took a deep breath. She was likely to be just as reluctant to meet him here in Oxford Street as she had been at home, but he could hardly walk by without acknowledging her existence. He closed the distance between them and cleared his throat.

"The fashions are getting more daring every year," he observed. She turned toward him with a little start.

"Oh, Lord William! Good afternoon. What a pleasure to see a friendly face." Despite the fact that she had repeatedly refused to see him at home, she truly did look happy to meet him. Her blue eyes were alight with good humor. He wondered how many unfriendly faces she had encountered during her stay in London.

"I was not sure whether you would be pleased to see me," he confessed. "You seemed most reluctant to receive me at your cousin's home."

Her smile was sheepish. "Please accept my apologies for my rudeness. For the last few days, I would have been reluctant to receive the Prince Regent. I have not been myself. But I have put all that behind me."

He raised his eyebrows. "Truly?"

She nodded. "Fretting in Mrs. Templeton's drawing room will not bring me any closer to my goal. I decided it was time to shake off my blue-devils. My cousin's husband is in trade in the City, and several of his business associates are joining us for dinner later this week. I thought it might be useful to pick up a few new ribbons for the occasion." She inclined her head toward the shop window.

He almost teased her by saying, "Just a few ribbons, and not an entirely new ensemble?" Then he realized that her budget likely didn't run to elaborate hats and gowns. She would need to make do with what she already owned. If the dresses she had worn at Larkwood and on the journey to London were any indication, she would be sadly out of fashion. Not as out of fashion as Lady Glenmont, perhaps, but still a dun sparrow in a world of bright parakeets.

It seemed the height of unfairness that she should be forced to troll through assemblies of dull Cits without even the minor pleasure of new clothes to cheer her. It was all due to George, he reminded himself. If she wasn't so devilish prickly, he would offer her enough money to buy a complete new wardrobe. Heaven knew, he certainly had the blunt. He lived frugally and had invested prudently.

He knew without a shadow of a doubt that any help he tried to provide would be thrown back in his face. Why did he care, anyway?

Responsibility and duty, he told himself, as he looked into her heart-shaped face. Well, those were the main reasons.

"What brings you to Oxford Street, my lord?" she asked.

"A few errands. Mainly, I just wanted to be outside enjoying this fine day." He waved a hand to indicate the abundant sunshine and the pansies blooming in a pot outside a modiste's shop.

"And is it pleasant, being out among people?" Her eyes were knowing. He wondered again how many barbs she had endured.

"I have no trouble," she added, as if she had seen into his mind. It was odd how often she seemed to read his thoughts before he had even registered them himself. "No one in London knows me, so I can slip through the streets unnoticed. But I suppose you have no such luxury."

He shook his head and smiled. "This is just a tempest in a teapot," he said, trying to reassure himself as much as her. "Next week, some other juicy tidbit will be served up for the *ton*'s delectation. A lady will be seen late at night in the company of a man not her husband, or a gentleman will lose his house in an ill-considered wager, and the affairs of the Duke of Cambermere will be very old news."

She straightened her shoulders and looked directly into his eyes. "My cousin tells me the same thing, and since you both know much more about London life than I do, it would be foolish not to believe you."

William glanced around and saw neither Lady Glenmont nor Mrs. Templeton. "Are you here alone?"

"No, my mother encountered an old acquaintance in the shoemaker's shop next door. They began to discuss . . . the affair . . . and I thought I might enjoy getting a little fresh air." She looked away, up the street.

The gossip was hurting her more than she let on. William began counting to ten, and realized it would do no good. He could count to a thousand, and his anger toward his foolish brother would not diminish one whit. What had the scoundrel been thinking, to give their mother's betrothal ring to an innocent young woman and then turn his back on her?

The betrothal ring. William had forgotten all about it. Suddenly, the perfect idea began taking shape in his mind.

"Lady Sarah, I know that you will need funds to purchase a few new gowns for your season in Town," he began.

"You think my gowns unseemly?" she asked, glancing down at her plain ensemble.

Dash it! He was a trained diplomat. Why could he not seem to avoid putting his foot in his mouth where Lady Sarah was concerned?

"Not at all. But I know what an extensive wardrobe most ladies bring to London for the Season, and I thought you might enjoy having some pretty new things."

"What I might enjoy and what is likely to happen are two different things, my lord." Her words were sharp, but her tone was sad.

"If you hope to snare the attentions of a gentleman, you must be dressed to hold your own in the marriage mart." As he spoke the words, he realized that she could hold her own in any assembly of women, even were she dressed in her ridiculous fencing costume. She was not conventionally beautiful, but there was something about her—wit, intelligence, strength, *something* that he couldn't quite define—that would set her apart and above the usual Incomparables of the Season, no matter how finely her rivals were garbed.

The problem was, if he told her that, she wouldn't believe him.

"I can help," he continued in a rush, before he could follow his line of thought any further.

Her eyes narrowed. "Lord William—"

He held up his hand to stall the inevitable protest. "Wait, it wouldn't be *I*. It would be George, in a way."

She stilled, and her silence gave him the confidence to go on.

"George gave you that emerald betrothal ring."

"Which I returned."

"But you shouldn't have," he said, warming to his theme. "By rights, George owes you the settlement he promised you. But we both know the battle to retrieve it would be expensive, embarrassing, and likely fruitless."

She nodded.

"But he *did* give you the ring, and by all rights you should have kept it. It was an installment payment, if you will, on the settlement that is legally yours."

As she considered his argument, she nibbled on her lower lip. For a moment, he forgot what he was about to say. Then he realized he was staring at her like a green schoolboy, and cleared his throat.

"So I propose that I return it to you. I can have it sent round to Paradise Row this very afternoon. I should never have accepted its return in the first place, but I wasn't thinking completely clearly in the circumstances that night."

She toyed with her reticule and glanced at the

ground as she considered his plan. For once, it seemed she might actually bend and accept some help.

"The goods in the shops here are very dear," she said finally.

"They are," he agreed, hope quickening in his chest. It was ridiculous, really, how much importance he was placing on her answer. She was no longer any concern of his. It should not matter whether she said yes or no.

"And I have never argued that Lord Cambermere was not legally in my debt."

"If the contract had been completed, no judge in the land would dispute that." Fleetingly, William recalled his brother's smug countenance as he'd described the paperwork burning in his solicitor's grate.

George had better stay in Italy a long, long time. It might take years before it would be safe for him to be in a room alone again with his brother.

Lady Sarah scuffed the toe of her half boot against the pavement, then seemed to come to a conclusion. "It does me no credit, but I must admit that it would be satisfying to recover something from your brother," she said with a small smile.

He blinked. He had actually cracked her facade. She was going to let him help her.

"I would be more than happy to press him to settle the full amount on you—"

She laughed. "Don't take a mile when I have ceded only an inch, Lord William. It could only hurt my opportunities in Town if your brother chose to write a few letters to some well-chosen acquaintances, letting them know that his pathetic former fiancée was badgering him for funds."

William felt a rush of admiration for her. She had been in Town less than a week, but she already understood the ways of the beau monde better than some young women who had been immersed in it for years.

"I suppose you are right. Can you just see the caricatures in the shop windows?"

She laughed—a surprisingly hearty laugh, considering the topic of their conversation. "Fortunately, Rowlandson and his cronies have no idea what I look like. Yet." She paused. "Are their likenesses of the new duchess accurate?" she asked in a hesitant voice.

William recalled the most famous one. Even though the picture was grossly exaggerated, the artist had captured Harriet's unmistakable beauty. The luxuriant coil of hair, her celebrated curves, the famous long line of her throat—they had all been reproduced faithfully. "As accurate as these things ever are," he said carefully.

"I suspected as much." Her voice was brisk. "Not that it is any affair of mine."

William's right hand clenched. As well as destroying her reputation, George appeared to have taken a small bit of Lady Sarah's confidence with him when he'd bolted.

"You must not blame yourself for George's idiocy. Believe me, you have far more to recommend you to a man than Harriet Partridge ever will," he blurted.

"Thank you for that, Lord William," she said with a bright smile that made him feel as though he had given her a tiara, a house, the moon. "It really has been good to see you today."

They stared at each other for a long moment. William was barely aware of the tumult of Oxford Street around them until a familiar voice pierced the odd cocoon that seemed to have been spun between himself and Lady Sarah.

"Lord William!" Lady Glenmont cried. He turned to see her emerging, with some difficulty, from a small shop. She eventually twisted sideways and sidled out the door left pannier first.

He bowed. "Good afternoon, Lady Glenmont. I trust you are enjoying your time in town?"

She nodded. "Most certainly. I have seen so many people I haven't seen in years." She looked toward Sarah. "Have you seen anything that catches your fancy, dear? I know you will protest that we cannot afford it, but I do think you should have a pretty new ensemble for Mary's dinner party. I would lend you one of my gowns, but I know they are not what the young women wear these days."

Lady Sarah smiled. "I do believe I will indulge myself in one or two new gowns, Mother. My concerns about our financial situation don't seem as strong as they once were." She glanced briefly at William.

So she did not plan to tell her mother about the ring. That was no concern of his.

Lady Glenmont clapped her hands together. "Thank goodness, Sally!" She turned to William. "I had just about despaired of getting her to wear anything but these dull dresses that don't show her off well at all. If we must attract a fortune, as Sally assures me we must—"

"There is no question about it," Lady Sarah put in with a tired sigh.

"—then she must be dressed for the part. One catches more flies with honey than with vinegar, as my mother used to say."

Lady Sarah looked away at this little speech, as well she might. It wasn't uncommon among the nobility to marry for money, but it was a bit disconcerting to hear them speak of it so openly.

"And I hope we catch you a charming fly, my dear," the countess continued, oblivious to her daughter's discomfort. "Mary tells me that Mr. Bellingham has a grand house in Shropshire, so he must be prosperous. And Mr. Taylor has investments in several trading companies doing business in the West Indies. Mary did not mention whether these gentlemen were fair of face, but I certainly hope they are, for your sake."

Lady Sarah's smile looked brittle. "Whether they are or not, I suppose it is time for us to visit the modiste's and begin gilding the lily." She slipped her hand through her mother's arm. "Good day, Lord William. And . . . thank you."

He bowed slightly as they moved away down the pavement, and he continued in the opposite direction.

It should not sicken him to hear the Harrisons discussing their plans. Lady Sarah had never made a secret of the fact that she had come to London with the express purpose of finding a wealthy husband. So why did his stomach twist as he realized that the money from his grandmother's ring would be used to help Lady Sarah land a moneyed Cit who likely had more interest in her titled family and her pretty clothes than in anything else about her? That was the way the marriage mart worked, after all.

It just did not seem right, for women to proffer themselves like choice biscuits for the delectation of any man with a heavy purse. It was one step up from—

William caught himself before he completed the thought. What Lady Sarah was doing was perfectly respectable.

It was just as well that he would soon be shot of London, he thought as he reached the stationer's shop. It would be far too disconcerting to keep running into Lady Sarah. She invariably took his mind off his work.

SEVEN

Sarah shifted position on the hard settee in Mrs. Templeton's salon. With effort, she resisted the urge to tuck her feet up under her skirts, curl into the upholstery, and go to sleep. How could simple conversation be so exhausting? Truly, fencing with Sam had been less wearing.

She had been sitting and smiling at a series of potential suitors for well over four hours. Her mother had retired to her room half an hour ago, fatigued by the long session, and Sarah longed to do the same.

Mrs. Templeton had explained that customary visiting hours among the *haut ton* were not normally so long, but men with business interests had other responsibilities and could not necessarily visit during traditional times. As a result, she had encouraged her husband's friends to pay calls at whatever time was most convenient.

They were an interesting assembly, to say the least. Sarah liked her cousin's bluff, boisterous spouse, who ran a drapery shop in the Strand. "Everyone said I was marrying beneath me when we wed, but I wouldn't have cared if he was a marquess or a merchant," Mrs. Templeton had told Sarah one afternoon between callers.

Sarah didn't like to think she was high in the instep, but she had to admit that none of the gentlemen who came to pay their respects to her had a fraction of Mr. Templeton's charm and manners. One had assured her that she looked like "a good breeder," while another had spent his entire visit boasting of his collection of birds' nests. A third had looked her up and down with such a leer that she had been delighted when he left after a two-minute visit. Obviously, she had not met with his approval, and that was quite fine with her.

"I'm sorry these last few callers have been such a sorry lot," Mrs. Templeton apologized, pouring Sarah another cup of tea. "I don't know what Thomas was thinking, truly I don't, to send that Mr. Francis here. He barely has two teeth in his head."

"He was the nicest of the group, despite his lack of teeth," Sarah said with a chuckle. "It's unfortunate that he was seeking a wife with a bit more experience in raising children. With eight little ones at home, I can understand his predicament." She added a small lump of sugar to her cup and stirred.

"What about Mr. Ross? He seemed very pleasant."

Sarah raised the teacup to her lips and sipped before replying. "I don't think you heard the remark he made to me just before he left. He said he hoped I appreciated the favor he was doing me in even coming to call." Despite her best intentions to stay optimistic, she felt weary. "I know I have said this before, but it is discouraging to be blamed for a state of affairs that is not of my making."

Mrs. Templeton clucked sympathetically. "I know,

dear. But neither you nor I can change the way Society thinks." She leaned forward, looked as though she were about to speak, then pressed her lips together.

"What is it, Mrs. Templeton? Please don't hesitate to speak freely. There is nothing you can say that the newspapers have not already published."

Her hostess looked at the floor. "Believe me, Sarah, I do not mean to criticize, but I know how much you want to find a husband quickly. And I think you need to be, well, a little less selective. You may need to focus more on the gentleman's purse than on his other attributes."

Sarah set down her cup and frowned.

"Oh dear, I've upset you! The very thing I did not want to do." Mrs. Templeton twisted her hands in her lap.

"No, no, you are absolutely correct," Sarah hastened to reassure her hostess. "And you were right to tell me. Sometimes, I simply forget the realities of the world I now inhabit."

She sighed. "The truth is, I will never find a man who is both rich and charming. Such men can have their pick of many women in London, and a lady with a reputation such as mine will not be able to compete. I have met several men who are charming but not rich," she said, trying to expunge the image of a certain stuffy dark-haired lord that suddenly formed in her mind. "Those gentlemen will not serve my purposes. I must turn my attention to men who are rich but not necessarily charming."

Mrs. Templeton reached across the small gap between their chairs and squeezed Sarah's hand. "I know it sounds harsh, Sarah, but it is for the best.

With luck, one of your callers will be a gentleman of character who has the courage to ignore the newspaper reports."

"Let's hope for luck," Sarah said bleakly as she selected a biscuit from the plate on the table and nibbled on it. Ever since this chore had begun, she had developed an insatiable craving for sweets. If she did not find a husband soon, she would have to add portliness to her list of deficiencies, and that would just make her more of a liability in the marriage mart.

Regretfully, she placed the remainder of the biscuit on her saucer.

Mrs. Templeton's butler opened the door and poked his head in. "Mr. Wolton is downstairs. Are you at home?"

"Yes, please show him in," Sarah's cousin replied, and the butler disappeared.

"I think you may like Mr. Wolton," Mrs. Templeton said as she turned back toward Sarah. "He's an investor, Thomas says. Made his fortune on the 'Change, although there's been some talk that some of his deals were somewhat suspect." She frowned.

"As you've just pointed out, I am in no position to dismiss any gentleman out of hand," Sarah said. "I'm sure Mr. Templeton would not have invited him if he were a true scoundrel."

"That's true, dear." Mrs. Templeton brightened. "He's much younger than some of these other gentlemen, and rather handsome, too, I daresay."

"I am looking forward to meeting him," Sarah replied, straightening her shoulders and trying to sound enthusiastic as the sound of footsteps on the stairs reached them. A few moments later, the door opened again and a tall gentleman strolled in. He wore an impeccably tailored jacket of dark green superfine, a snowy neckcloth, and spotless buff pantaloons—everything in the latest stare of fashion, without being showy in Chadwick's manner.

"Good afternoon, Mr. Wolton," her hostess said as their guest walked over to her chair. "May I introduce you to my cousin, Lady Sarah Harrison?"

He turned his attention to Sarah and smiled. Without even needing to make an effort, she smiled back.

He had a pleasant face with a square jaw and the hint of a dimple in his right cheek. Small patches of gray at his temples made him look distinguished, but when she studied his face for a moment, Sarah divined that he was going gray at a young age. There were few hints of lines around his eyes or across his smooth forehead.

"I am pleased to make your acquaintance, Lady Sarah," he said with a small bow.

"I am delighted to meet you as well, sir," she said, realizing as she mouthed the words that she actually meant them. Perhaps he had made a few unsavory bargains at the 'Change, she thought. But who was she to cast the first stone?

"Mr. Templeton tells me you hail from Yorkshire," he said, settling into a Queen Anne chair and accepting the cup of tea Mrs. Templeton poured for him.

"Yes. This is my first visit to London." That admission didn't shame her as it had when she had made it to Lord William.

"And how do you like the capital so far?" He observed her from keen gray eyes that she suspected missed little.

"Very much. Yesterday we visited Astley's Circus, and I found it most entertaining. There is little opportunity to see acrobats in Yorkshire."

He chuckled. "I am glad you enjoyed it. It has been many years since I've been to Astley's Circus myself."

They chatted for several minutes about inconsequential topics. Then, as Sarah had learned was the custom in Town, Mr. Wolton stood to take his leave. After a week in the city, she was finally becoming accustomed to these very short visits. Out in the country, visitors always stayed at least a few hours—there was little point driving miles across the fields just to drink one cup of tea and depart.

She had been rather pleased to see the vast majority of her visitors leave. But in the case of Mr. Wolton, she was sorry that his visit was so short. He seemed a very pleasant gentleman.

"Please come back and visit again," she said as he bid them farewell. Immediately, she could have bitten off her tongue. She probably sounded desperate.

If he thought the same, he gave no indication. "It would be my pleasure. But in the meantime, would you be interested in accompanying me for a drive in Hyde Park next Tuesday?"

Sarah hoped her face did not betray the relief she felt. She had been certain he would be one of the gentlemen who left his card and did not call again. "Thank you, Mr. Wolton. I would be delighted."

He took his leave, and she leaned against the back of the settee. Finally, after a week of drinking tea and making bright conversation, she seemed to have attracted the attention of a potential suitor.

And none too soon. Her father's latest letter had made it clear that a few of their creditors were becoming increasingly impatient. Imploring her not to tell her mother, he had admitted that he had pawned his mother's silver platter and an old branch of candlesticks in order to repay the burly man who had supplied some of the marble he had used to build the gazebo a decade ago.

It was only fair. In any case, if I had not, I believe he would have attempted to publicize the debt more widely. Given the choice between selling the silver and falling into local disrepute, I think your mother would have far preferred that I do the former, he had written.

Her cousin crossed the floor to the window. "Well done, Sarah!" she exclaimed as she peered through a gap in the curtains. "He has a very elegant phaeton—bright blue, with a pretty white horse. I am sure you will have a most enjoyable drive in the park."

"I know we will," said Sarah, her heart pounding. She had not realized how much she had feared failure today until Mr. Wolton extended his invitation.

If she were lucky, one of her new day dresses would be ready in time for their drive. And perhaps she would ask Mrs. Templeton's lady's maid to dress her hair a bit more elaborately.

She closed her eyes and took a deep breath. So much depended on this one carriage ride.

William reined in Midnight as a carriage suddenly veered in front of him to pull alongside a gilt-edged curricle. Evidently, the elegantly coiffed women sitting beside their escorts in each conveyance had something of vital import to say to each other that justified their taking up most of the roadway.

He sighed. Normally, he avoided Hyde Park at the fashionable hour. But he had been occupied in meetings at Whitehall all day, and when he had emerged late in the afternoon and had caught a whiff of rose blooms in the air, he had been unwilling to retire to his stuffy rooms or to the dimness of White's. It had been days since he had taken Midnight out just for pleasure. On a day like this, the lure of the outdoors was irresistible.

A month ago, even, the park would have been crowded but bearable. But the Season was in full swing, and more people were pouring into London every day for the victory celebrations. People who hadn't been to Town in years had opened up their neglected town houses and dusted off their finery in the hopes of being invited to one of the glittering fetes being given in honor of the Czar's visit. The city had an unmistakable energy these days.

William himself felt more energetic than he had in quite some time. This afternoon, Castlereagh had asked him to be part of a small advance party of diplomatic representatives who would go to the site of the peace talks—which still looked likely to be Vienna—in advance of the actual negotiations. They would take part in some preliminary discussions with other parties and arrange lodgings and other services for the larger delegation. It was still unclear when he would need to leave, but by early fall he would likely be on his way for an extended trip abroad. He could hardly wait.

When it became clear that the two carriage drivers intended to stay stopped in the middle of the road for quite some time, William spurred Midnight into a gentle trot and guided her into the verge. He had just drawn the horse up onto the road again, on the other side of the stationary vehicles, when he heard a familiar voice call his name. He scanned the colorful assemblage of carriages and mounted riders.

Coming toward him on the right was a blue high-perch phaeton. On one side, Lady Sarah was waving with unmistakable enthusiasm. He grinned as he recognized her. London might be a grand city, the largest in the world, but the *ton* certainly moved in small circles.

His smile faded as his eyes traveled to the driver of the carriage. Of all the people he would have hoped to see squiring Lady Sarah about Town, Henry Wolton was last on the list.

It had been several years since William had had the misfortune to encounter Wolton. In the interim, the man had changed little. He was still as elegant as ever, living proof of the old cliché that you couldn't tell a book by its cover. Both William and George had been taken in by the smooth-talking entrepreneur, although William had realized their mistake and had warned George before his brother had invested too much money in Wolton's ill-conceived mining scheme.

True, Wolton had never done anything precisely illegal. Even on moral grounds, it was hard to fault him. It was just that he rarely told the entire truth about any of his ventures, and he preyed on the gullible and the weak.

From Wolton's narrowed eyes, it was clear that he was as displeased to see William as William was to see him. But when Wolton glanced at Lady Sarah and saw her obvious delight, his expression became a bland mask.

Obviously, he was trying to impress the lady. It made sense that Wolton would pursue Lady Sarah, William thought as he reined in Midnight once more. The trader was a very wealthy man who had no need to marry a large dowry—although William was certain he would not decline one were it offered. What Wolton needed, if he was ever to maintain the trust of the *haut ton* who were his main investors, was respectability. And despite his debt, Lord Glenmont was heir to one of England's oldest titles. The Glenmonts may have been poor money managers, but until George had cried off from his betrothal to Lady Sarah, not a whiff of scandal had ever attached itself to the family.

William caught himself up short at that thought. Surely Wolton had heard of Lady Sarah's jilting? A man would have had to be deaf and blind not to have caught wind of it by now.

Perhaps he was staking his bets on the fact that her disgrace would eventually be forgotten in the light of the next society bumblebroth, and he wanted to make sure he was at the front of the line for her affections—or at least, her name—when the gossip died down.

That sounded right. Wolton was noted for his patience in laying traps. It only stood to reason that he would be patient in waiting for a rare prize like an earl's daughter. It would be a long time before another lady of quality gave him a second glance. Most of the members of the *haut ton* who spent much time in Town gave him a wide berth.

He reined in Midnight. "Good afternoon, Lady Sarah, Mr. Wolton. You have picked a particularly lovely day for a drive."

Wolton nodded. "Cates. It has been a long time." His voice was flat. It was clear that any conversation between them would be perfunctory, which suited William admirably.

"You are looking very pretty today, Lady Sarah," William said, turning his attention back to her. And indeed she was. She wore a silk dress of an appealing shade that he believed was called bottle green and had opened a matching parasol above her head. Her gown was cut in a more fashionable style than the simple dresses she had worn on their journey to London, and he could not help but notice that it showed off her slim arms—and a great deal else—to advantage. Her modiste was to be commended. "Is that a new dress?"

Her smile showed that she understood the full import of the question and that she didn't bear him any ill will for persuading her to accept the return of the betrothal ring. "It is. In a way, it was the gift of a kind friend."

He basked in the warmth of her regard, even as a small, mean part of him resented the fact that she had used the profits from the ring to buy finery to attract the likes of Wolton. Was there any way he could discreetly warn her away from the investor? Not at the moment, certainly, but perhaps in the future.

She will not welcome your advice, let alone take it, he reminded himself sternly.

They spoke of inconsequential topics for several minutes as the traffic of Hyde Park flowed around them. Then Wolton hailed a gentleman passing on the opposite side of the phaeton, who reined in his horse. After some brief introductions, Wolton and his acquaintance fell into a deep discussion of a horse the other man was considering purchasing. When William was certain that Wolton was sufficiently distracted, he leaned down and placed his lips close to Lady Sarah's ear. He caught a faint scent of oranges and cinnamon. She must have been using some exotic preparation in her toilette.

"Lady Sarah," he whispered, praying that Wolton wouldn't hear. "Be very cautious in your dealings with Mr. Wolton. His reputation is not precisely spotless."

She moved her head away to look him fully in the face. Her blue eyes were wide and, he had to admit, not terribly friendly. With a sideways glance at her companion, who was still deep in conversation with the gentleman on horseback, she motioned William to turn his head so that she could reply.

"That may be so, Lord William, but I am not exactly in a position to be selective, as someone reminded me not so long ago."

He grimaced. "I realize that your circumstances are somewhat precarious, and I did not mean to interfere," he whispered. "As a friend, I am simply warning you to be careful."

She nodded. "I shall, and I thank you." Despite her words, he sensed that she would be very unlikely to discourage any attentions Wolton deigned to pay her. And he could not blame her, really. The torrent of newspaper coverage had probably reduced the pool of gentlemen likely to pay her serious attention to a mere puddle.

At that moment, Wolton concluded his conversation. His acquaintance wheeled his horse and trotted off along the road, and Wolton twisted back in his

We'd Like to Invite You to Subscribe to Zebra's Regency Romance Book Club and Send You 4 Free Books as Your Introduction! (Worth $19.96!)

If you're a Regency lover, imagine the joy of getting 4 FREE Zebra Regency Romances and then the chance to have these lovely stories delivered to your home each month at the lowest price available! Well, that's our offer to you and here's how you benefit by becoming a Regency Romance subscriber:

- *4 FREE Introductory Regency Romances are delivered to your doorstep (you only pay for shipping & handling)*

- *4 BRAND NEW Regencies are then delivered each month (usually before they're available in bookstores)*

- *Subscribers save almost $4.00 off the cover price every month*

- *You also receive a FREE monthly newsletter, which features author profiles, discounts, subscriber benefits, book previews and more*

- *There's no risks or obligations...in other words, you can cancel whenever you wish with no questions asked*

Join the thousands of readers who enjoy the savings and convenience offered to Regency Romance subscribers. After your initial introductory shipment, you'll receive 4 brand-new Zebra Regency Romances each month to examine for 10 days. Then, if you decide to keep the books, you pay the preferred subscriber's price, plus shipping and handling.

It's a no-lose proposition, so return the FREE BOOK CERTIFICATE today!

Treat yourself to 4 FREE Regency Romances!
A $19.96 VALUE... FREE!
No obligation to buy anything ever!

REGENCY ROMANCE BOOK CLUB
Zebra Home Subscription Service, Inc.
P.O. Box 5214
Clifton NJ 07015-5214

seat. "Well, Lady Sarah, shall we proceed?" He shot a suspicious look at William.

Touché, William thought. Wolton had already divined that William was not supportive of any designs the trader might have on Lady Sarah. Well, the man had not become fabulously wealthy by being stupid.

"I was just on my way as well," William said with a brief nod at Wolton and a quick glance at Lady Sarah. She still looked somewhat mutinous, but at least he had put some doubts about Wolton in her mind. With luck, that would be enough to stop her from doing anything truly foolish.

He spurred Midnight into a brisk trot and continued down the road. Keeping an eye on Lady Sarah would likely be a substantial occupation over the next few months. Although why he felt the need to—

He cut off his own thoughts in midstream. There was no point remonstrating with himself about his continued interest in the earl's daughter. He had tried many times to stop thinking about her and failed every time. He simply had to accept the fact that, while she was in London at least, he would feel in some way responsible for her. He would do his best to help her, while ensuring that his efforts did not overwhelm his other, more important concerns—such as the upcoming talks in Vienna.

That was a cheering thought. The debacle with George did not seem to have affected Castlereagh's confidence in William's ability to maintain respect and wield authority in the diplomatic community, thank heaven. Within a few months, if he was lucky, he would be shot of London, and far from any worries about George, Harriet, or Lady Sarah.

That day could not come too soon.

EIGHT

Sarah paused in the midst of a letter she was writing to Hester. It was oddly quiet in the Templetons' house today. Mrs. Templeton and Lady Glenmont had gone to visit friends, leaving Sarah to cope with anyone who might come to call. She had rather hoped that Mr. Wolton would visit, but there had been no sign of him. And the few other gentlemen who had initially visited at Mr. Templeton's urgings had not maintained their interest. Even Mr. Francis—the man of few teeth—had not made a reappearance.

She sighed. Even though she would have gladly entertained the other gentlemen for the sake of their fortunes, she was happy to have been spared the obligation. But she had rather hoped that Mr. Wolton would pay a call. He had said he would try, but he had warned her that he had a number of other business engagements to attend to that might consume most of his time today.

Despite Lord William's warnings, and some additional information on Mr. Wolton's background that Mr. Templeton had reluctantly yielded over dinner one night, Sarah still held out hope that she and the trader could make a suitable match. She held no illusions that it would be anything but a business arrangement, and neither did he. They should suit each other's interests admirably.

She had been on several outings with the merchant since their initial drive in Hyde Park. They had attended a musicale at the home of one of Mrs. Templeton's friends, and they had been part of a group that had taken a picnic to Hampstead Heath. Mrs. Templeton had urged her to invite him to supper tomorrow evening, if he happened to call today.

Sarah returned her attention to her letter. She had finished the missive to Hester and begun a letter to Chadwick at Oxford when the Templetons' butler knocked at the door.

"Lady Sarah, you have a caller."

"Excellent," she replied, putting down her quill and wiping the tips of her somewhat inky fingers on a small rag.

"It is Lord William Cates. Shall I show him in?"

Lord William? Sarah hesitated. It had been more than a week since she had encountered the duke's brother in Hyde Park, and she had begun to hope that he had finally shaken any interest in protecting her. She was doing rather well on her own, she thought.

But it would be churlish to refuse to see him. What harm was there in it, after all? None that she could see.

"Please do, Seward."

Within moments, she heard his light tread on the stairs. The door opened again and he entered. "Good afternoon, Lady Sarah," he said, crossing the room to greet her.

"It is lovely to see you, Lord William. May I offer you some refreshment?"

"I would not say no. It is growing rather warm outside, and I must confess that I am rather thirsty."

Sarah dispatched Seward to alert the housekeeper that they were in need of a tea tray, then stood and moved to the settee before the fireplace.

"It is pleasant to see you, Lord William." As she said the words, she realized they were true. She might resent his interference in her affairs, but that did not mean she could not enjoy his company.

He leaned back in his chair and stretched out his legs. As always, he was flawlessly attired. Today he was wearing buff pantaloons and a deep blue jacket, with his usual expertly tied neckcloth. She tried, and failed, to ignore how well his garments showed off his legs to advantage and how much fitter Lord William appeared than the rather portly Mr. Wolton.

"You are looking most fetching today, Lady Sarah," he replied, eyeing her yellow day dress. "It appears you have invested your clothing budget most sensibly. That gown becomes you very well."

"Thank you." To her annoyance, she felt a slight heat rising on her cheeks. Really, was she such a country miss that she could not even accept a simple compliment without blushing? With determination, she steered the conversation away from herself. "Have you received any further news of a posting abroad?"

"I have indeed," he said with a smile as a young housemaid bustled in with a tea tray and set it on the low Sheraton table. "It appears that I shall be sent to Vienna by the end of the summer."

"That soon?" she said without thinking, and then could have bitten off her tongue. The last thing she needed was for Lord William to think she could not get along without him. Although that hadn't been what she was thinking at all. She was simply reflecting that she would miss him.

It was natural enough, she told herself. She knew almost no one in London. The thought of one of her few acquaintances leaving Town was bound to be distressing.

He smiled. "The season is young yet, Lady Sarah. In fact, I have come today to invite you to enjoy an entertainment with me. Would you be interested in accompanying me to see the procession tomorrow?"

"A procession?"

"To celebrate the arrival of Czar Alexander and the other Allied leaders in London. Through my work at Whitehall, I can secure us an excellent vantage point." He adjusted his cuffs. "And in the evening, a colleague of mine is hosting a small soiree in honor of the occasion, with a light supper and dancing. Fortunately, he is not too high in the instep to invite me, despite George's antics. You would be most welcome as well."

Her mind raced ahead. Why on earth would he want to squire her about on a social occasion? Surely he was not still planning to press his suit on her, was he?

As though he had read her mind, he continued. "I would be escorting you merely as a friend, I assure you. It occurred to me that it was foolish to simply warn you away from Wolton without trying to provide you with any suitable alternatives. Gen-

tlemen from across the social spectrum will be view-
ing the procession from our enclosure, and
chances are great that we will run into many
wealthy gentlemen to whom I could introduce you.
And there may be several likely candidates at
Arthur's soiree. The members of the foreign office
aren't known for their deep pockets, but Arthur's
wife is a noted hostess and knows all sorts of people." He sighed and pulled his arms above his head,
which stretched his fine lawn shirt across his chest
in a most distracting manner. For a brief instant,
Sarah recalled how Lord William had looked that
afternoon in the barn at Larkwood, grinning in his
shirtsleeves, his hair damp with perspiration.

She realized he had finished speaking and was
waiting patiently for her response.

Did she want to go to this parade with him? Yes,
very much, she realized, which was exactly the reason why she should decline. "Thank you very much
for your kind offer," she began.

"Please don't deny me this small pleasure," he cut
in with a wide grin, leaning forward.

He really shouldn't smile like that. It wasn't quite
fair. It almost looked as though he actually wanted
to go on this outing, instead of considering it a family duty.

"I know you only want to help me, but truly, I am
managing quite well on my own."

"Then you have found other suitors besides Mr.
Wolton?" His voice had a very slightly mocking
edge to it, and she bristled.

"Yes, of course," she snapped. "There is Mr.
Archibald Francis, for example."

Lord William laughed. "I meant suitors with *teeth*."

Despite herself, she felt an answering grin tugging at the corners of her mouth. "Their teeth mean nothing to me. It is only their purses I am interested in, as you well know."

"And I could certainly help you find a gentleman with both teeth and blunt," he replied. He reached across the small gap between them and gently took her hand. "Please let me help you. I know I should just walk away and leave you to your fate, as you have so often asked me to do, but I simply seem unable to do so. I know that you would fare wonderfully on your own. Believe me, I don't doubt that you could do just about anything, if you put your mind to it." He squeezed her hand. "I just want to make the road a little easier. Humor me, please."

Lord William's pretty little speech was almost lost on Sarah, as every nerve and thought in her body seemed to focus on the sensation of her hand in his. His grip was strong and comforting. For a man who so often seemed cool and reserved, his palm was as warm as a fireside in December.

He squeezed her hand.

"Yes, yes of course, Lord William," she heard herself murmuring stupidly. "Attending the procession and your friend's soiree is a wonderful idea."

No, it wasn't. It was a ridiculous idea. The last thing she needed was to spend more time with Lord William. All he did was send her mind wandering down pointless paths.

His answering smile was wistful. "I wish I could escort you to Almack's, but George's reckless behavior has made me persona non grata there at the minute, I'm afraid. Have you tried to get vouchers yourself?"

She nodded. "To no avail. It seems that one of the patronesses has deemed me beyond the pale as well."

"They're terribly hypocritical," Lord William said, his voice terse. "There is barely a soul in those rooms on any given night who does not harbor a secret he would prefer to hide from public view. And most of those secrets are far more incriminating than your affair. After all, you were just an innocent bystander, while many of those men who hold their heads so high at Almack's—"

"Please," she interrupted him. "It does not bother me, truly. My family has never been interested in social prominence, and so it does not bother me in the slightest that a group of pompous hostesses has examined me and found me wanting."

Lord William's smile was slow and admiring, and a tiny part of her delighted in his approval. "You are remarkably self-possessed, as I believe I mentioned when we first met."

She lifted the teapot and began to pour. "With a family such as mine, it is a useful skill. One doesn't go far abroad with my mother without becoming used to hearing a few whispers behind one's back." She set the teapot back on the tray with a clatter. "I did not mean to denigrate Mother, of course! I love her dearly."

"I know that." Lord William's voice was soothing. "But it is an undeniable fact that she does attract attention wherever she goes."

Sarah was relieved that he had not misunderstood. "She does, but the comfort she derives from dressing as she does far outweighs any minor embarrassment I may suffer as a result." She picked up the cup of tea she had poured and offered it to Lord William.

"Please do not answer if you feel my question intrusive, but why does she dress in that manner?" he asked as he accepted the cup.

"You are not being intrusive. It is a natural question." She poured herself a cup of tea and added a lump of sugar before continuing.

"I am my mother's fourth child," she began. "Her first three children all died in infancy. The first, Edward, passed away just days after he was born. The second, Louisa, tumbled down the main staircase at Larkwood at the age of two, and her twin, Emma, succumbed to a fever a few months later while my mother was increasing with me." Sarah sighed. No matter how often she told this story, it still filled her with sadness for her parents' loss. It was no wonder her father had escaped the dismal atmosphere of the house by building his follies, or that her mother had retreated into what she imagined was a happier time.

"As my father explained it to me, my mother was going through some storage trunks at Larkwood when she came across some old gowns that had belonged to her grandmother. She told my father that night how many happy visits she had spent with her grandmother as a child. The next evening, she came to dinner dressed in one of Lady Farnham's old gowns. Father says it was the first time he had seen her smiling since their third child had passed away. It cheered her and he could not see that it harmed anyone, so he said nothing and let her continue wearing her grandmother's old clothes."

She cast a glance at Lord William to see what his reaction was to this admittedly odd story, and saw nothing but kindness on his face. Bolstered, she continued.

"As the years went on, of course, many of my grandmother's gowns fell into disrepair. Fortunately, a seamstress in the village found it amusing to continue to make dresses in the old style. She said it was an interesting challenge, since the gowns today are comparatively simple. And, of course, my mother paid her handsomely for her trouble." Well, offered to pay her handsomely. Mrs. Little was just one of their many creditors who had become aware of the sorry state of the Harrisons' finances by now.

Lord William nodded. "Does she still wear the clothes out of sadness?"

Sarah considered the question. "Partly, I think. I did not know her before the tragedies, but Father says she was much livelier as a girl. There is always this sort of vague melancholy surrounding her, although she does her best to dispel it. But I think the old-fashioned clothes have simply become a habit with her now. When I was younger, I tried to convince her to adopt more fashionable styles, but she would have none of it. And I believe I like her best this way, in any case. She would not be my mother if she were dressed any differently. If everyone were a slave to conformity, the world would be a much less interesting place, I suspect."

"You may be right," said Lord William, an odd expression on his handsome features. He placed his cup on the side table and checked the watch that hung from a long fob. "I do not want to overstay my welcome, Lady Sarah, so I shall take my leave. Thank you for the refreshment. Shall I come for you at noon tomorrow?" He smiled as he stood.

"Yes, that would be lovely," Sarah said. "It was good to see you, Lord William."

She wondered whether he would bend over her hand and kiss it, as he had done when they had first arrived in London, but she suspected that that had been a rather formal show put on mostly for her mother and Mrs. Templeton's benefit. And, indeed, he bowed very correctly to her and moved toward the door.

She stifled a surge of regret. What a silly goose she had become! She no more wanted a kiss on the hand from Lord William than she had wanted his offer of marriage. The longer she stayed in London, the less she understood herself, she thought as she watched Lord William take his leave.

Just after eleven o'clock the following morning, William stood before the mirror in his dressing room, frowning.

"Is there sufficient starch in this neckcloth, Stinson?" he asked, adjusting the oriental knot and wondering whether he should have gone with a plainer knot instead.

"I used the customary amount, my lord," replied Stinson, returning from the wardrobe with a copper-colored waistcoat. "If it is not to your liking, I can fetch another."

"No, it is no matter." William gave up fussing with the neckcloth and held his arms out so the valet could put the waistcoat over his shoulders. It was foolish, really, to be fussing so much about his attire for this outing with Lady Sarah. It was not as though he were paying court to her, after all.

But he did feel something special for her, he admitted to himself as Stinson slipped the right arm of the waistcoat over a new shirt from Weston that had just been delivered that morning. It was pointless to pretend he was unaffected by her.

If the world were different, he might well be interested in courting her in earnest. She was just so different from the milk-and-water misses one encountered everywhere else in Town. He smiled as he recalled that George had once used just that expression in relation to Lady Sarah.

Whiskey-and-fire minx would be a far more apropos description, he thought as he slid his other arm into the waistcoat and began to button it.

He rarely wore this garment, finding it a bit too showy for his tastes. But a woman in a shop had once told him it flattered him, which was why he had asked Stinson to excavate it from the back of the wardrobe yesterday and freshen it up for today's outing.

"Good to see you wearing that waistcoat again, Lord William," said the valet, holding up a dark coat. "I'm sure Lady Sarah will find nothing to fault in your appearance." The normally expressionless valet seemed to be suppressing a smile as William put on the outer garment and straightened it across his shoulders.

William tried to give his servant a quelling

glance, but he was certain it would do no good. The valet knew him far too well.

"I'm sure you are right. You have done a marvelous job of equipping me to face the world, Stinson." William picked up his hat from a nearby table and jammed it on his head.

He walked the short distance to Cambermere House to once again avail himself of one of George's carriages. There were a number of advantages to his brother being out of the country, and free rein over his excellent stables was one of them.

The head groom greeted him with a familiar smile. "'Tis good you are here to give the horses some exercise," Richards said as he led the team and curricle into the stable yard. One of George's tigers was already ensconced on the back. "You did request the curricle, correct?"

"Yes—I wish to drive myself, and it's too fine a day to be cooped up in the landau."

"Where are you off to this afternoon? Will you be watching the parade, then?"

"Yes," William said, vaulting into the carriage. Richards had left the hood folded back in order that they might enjoy the air. "I shall be escorting Lady Sarah Harrison, and we will be attending a supper and soiree in the evening. It may be late before I return with the carriage."

Richards raised his eyebrows. He had been at Cambermere House since William's childhood, and he took a few more liberties with the Cates family than did most servants. "That is very kind of you, to invite Lady Sarah to the festivities."

"Nothing kind about it at all," William said as he

gathered up the reins. "She is a lovely young woman, and I am most pleased to be spending the day in her company."

He could almost see Richards bursting in his anxiety to go and spread this latest bit of news among the Cambermere House staff. Richards was a far more avid gossip than any *ton* grande dame. One might as well publish a notice in the *Times* as tell him anything.

Good, thought William as he clucked to the horses, and the carriage slowly began to move. It could only help Lady Sarah's reputation to have it bruited about in Mayfair—even if only by the servants—that she was attending major social events. Any small step he could take toward repairing her reputation would help.

The streets were crowded with every sort of vehicle, from elegant barouches occupied by elderly matrons to hay wagons overflowing with excited children. Everyone, it seemed, had come to Town to see the victors of the war against Napoleon.

William muttered under his breath as, three streets away from Cambermere House, he found himself stopped dead in a cluster of vehicles that seemed to stretch for miles in every direction. At this rate, the parade would be over before he even reached Chelsea. He tapped his crop against the edge of the carriage and frowned.

Fortunately, the clot of carriages did not take long to disperse, with most heading toward Hyde Park. Luckily, William's destination lay in the opposite direction, and so he arrived only a few minutes late to collect Lady Sarah.

She must have been watching for his arrival from

the front window, because she emerged from the town house shortly after the carriage rolled to a stop and he had jumped down from the seat.

As she hastened down the steps, he noticed that she was wearing yet another gown he had not seen before, this one a cheerful purple muslin sprigged with small flowers. It clung to her small frame in a most becoming way. In her hand, she carried a large straw hat.

"I do apologize for my tardiness," he said as he handed her up into the carriage.

"Do not give it a moment's thought. Mother and Mrs. Templeton just returned home from an attempt to visit Oxford Street—they gave up after it took them an hour just to reach the King's Road."

"Well, I hope we will not be similarly delayed. I would like to get to Hyde Park long before the royal visitors do."

"If we do not arrive on time, it is no matter," she said airily, fastening the hat to her head with a wide silk ribbon. "I am just happy to be out enjoying this lovely day. And I am certain that, in your line of work, you have had your fill of watching kings and generals strut about."

He laughed. She really was most irreverent. "But there are several gentlemen attending the parade who are most anxious to meet you."

She frowned. "That is true. For a moment, I almost forgot the point of this exercise." Her face brightened. "Will they also be attending the soiree?"

He nodded.

"Well then! Let's do our best to reach Hyde Park on time, but not fret if we don't. We will be able to see everyone this evening, so there's no sense worrying. It's too delightful a day to be concerned about small matters."

She had a point, he thought, recalling his earlier frustration in traffic. It was not always necessary for life to proceed exactly according to a plan.

"On a day like this, I can almost pretend I'm back out in the country again, as the air smells so fresh," she added.

Suddenly, he had an idea.

"Are you truly indifferent to seeing the procession?" he asked.

"I would be happy to see it, but my life shall be far from incomplete if I don't." She smiled.

"Would you prefer a ride in the country?"

Her eyes lit up. "But where? Would it not take us hours to escape London?"

He shook his head. "All the people are heading toward Hyde Park. But we could go in the opposite direction, to Richmond. The park there is huge and lovely. One may even see deer."

Her open smile made him feel like a magician. He felt as though he had given her a rare jewel instead of a simple offer of a drive in the country.

"Yes, Lord William, that would be lovely! I must confess, the thought of fighting through such crowds had started to seem overwhelming. I had no idea there would be so many people."

"The advantage to this plan is that Richmond will be rather deserted. Everyone will have come into Town for the festivities instead." The more he discussed the idea, the more appealing it seemed. Particularly because it had been years since he had given in to a spur-of-the-moment whim.

Thus resolved, he tugged on the reins and turned the carriage west toward Richmond. Within minutes, they had left the chaos of the London crowds far behind.

"Thank you so much for suggesting this outing, Lord William," she said as they strolled along a gravel path flanked with colorful herbaceous borders, the duke's tiger trailing behind at a respectful distance. As Lord William had predicted, the gardens were nearly deserted. It was almost like being back on the grounds at Larkwood.

Thoughts of Larkwood stabbed her with a tiny pinprick of guilt. What business had she to be enjoying herself out in the country, when her duty was to find a gentleman to extract her family from impending disaster? If they had gone to the parade as planned, who knows what sort of pinks of the *ton* she might have met?

Firmly, Sarah pushed such thoughts from her mind. Long ago, she had learned to stand by her decisions and to smother regrets. She had spent many nights feeling guilty that she had not urged her parents to stop spending, and countless more hours berating herself for not working harder, earlier, to find a suitable husband. Those thoughts had almost paralyzed her from taking action of any sort.

So she would stop second-guessing her decision to come to Richmond with Lord William, she resolved. Perhaps this interlude of sunshine and relaxed conversation would help her face the evening of socializing ahead with better grace. Lord William seemed to be looking forward to the small dinner party, but Sarah was dreading it. It would be another night of smiling at people she didn't know and pretending to understand the intricate workings of Town society. But it was all in a good cause, she reminded herself. And it behooved her to try her best tonight, as Lord William had been very kind to invite her.

"A penny for your thoughts, Lady Sarah?" he asked, smiling down at her.

She didn't want to tell him her missish fears about the evening to come. So instead, she brought up another subject that had been on her mind as they strolled the gardens. "I feel rather guilty that you have missed spending the afternoon with your friends, all in an effort to amuse me."

He began to wave aside her concerns, but she plunged ahead.

"I can't imagine that a simple garden stroll can hold a candle to the excitement you are missing at Hyde Park right now," she continued. "Is there anything here in Richmond that you would prefer to do?"

An odd light came into his eyes as he continued to look down at her. For a moment, she was embarrassed, although she didn't know why. But the expression passed from his face almost as quickly as it had appeared, and she wondered if she had imagined it.

"Truly, I am enjoying our afternoon," he said. "But is there anything else *you* would like to do? We still have an hour or so before we need return to Town. There is a very pretty path along the Thames, not far from here, that might make a diverting excursion."

She agreed that that would be most enjoyable, reflecting as she did that Lord William rarely expressed a wish of his own. On the other hand, when Mr. Wolton suggested an outing, he rarely asked whether she would enjoy it. He simply invited her and assumed she would be interested in the pastime because he was.

Lord William really should be more assertive about his own likes and dislikes, she thought as they reached the spot where they had left the carriage in the care of a local boy, who hurried to untie the horses as soon as he saw them approach. Lord William gave the child a coin, then turned to hand Sarah into the carriage.

She steeled herself against the jolt of awareness that always surged through her at his touch and stepped lightly into the vehicle, releasing his hand as soon as was proper. She smiled at him as he vaulted into the seat next to her. The tiger clambered onto the back of the vehicle, and they began what turned out to be a short drive.

As they drove, the bright sunshine dimmed. Sarah looked up to see a large, dark cloud trailing thick tendrils across the sun.

"It looks as though our lovely weather may be coming to an end," she remarked. "Although much of the sky is still blue. I can't imagine that any rain would last long."

"All the same, I'll have the tiger raise the hood and cover the carriage while we're on our walk," Lord William remarked, turning to give that instruction to the young boy.

Within a few minutes, they had arrived at the river. The tiger stayed behind to fuss with the carriage cover, promising to catch up with his passengers as soon as he was finished. Sarah and Lord William then set off in the direction of Cholmondeley Walk.

Once they had made their way to the riverside, Sarah could understand why Lord William had suggested this side trip. The views of the Thames from the path were lovely. She could scarcely believe they were only a short trip from the bustle of London.

"It is thanks to the Richmond Vestry that we are able to enjoy this view," he remarked as he offered her his arm. She tucked her hand behind his elbow, but carefully kept her distance as much as possible. He fairly radiated warmth. And even through the thick fabric of his coat, she could feel the tautness of his forearm. It reminded her all too vividly of the masculine picture he had presented the day they had fenced at Larkwood.

"How did the Richmond Vestry help?" she asked brightly as they set off along the path. Beside them, water burbled over submerged rocks and swirled in little eddies around bunches of weeds. The croaking of unseen frogs filled the air.

"The late Duke of Queensberry, who owned the property along Cholmondeley Walk, tried to limit public access to the path," Lord William explained. "The vestry, to its credit, took him to court."

Sarah raised her eyebrows. "But I thought no one says no to a duke."

Lord William looked at her and barked with laughter. His whole face lit up with mirth, and she couldn't help but join him. "I see that George managed to impart his personal philosophy to you during your brief acquaintance," he said finally.

She nodded. "That, and 'Never play faro with Lord Parkton, because he cheats.'"

Lord William chuckled again. "A regular Socrates, my brother."

It was good they could laugh about the whole debacle now, she thought as they continued their stroll. If even she could put it behind her, perhaps the rest of the *ton* had, too.

"So who owns the land now?" she asked as they came around a bend and caught sight of a grand stone bridge crossing the river.

"The Marquess of Hertford. Now there's an interesting story. Did you know that his wife was Queensberry's illegitimate daughter?"

Sarah shook her head.

"Despite that, she managed to marry a marquess and inherit all of Queensberry's property. So, you see, one bit of unseemly gossip does not ruin one's life in the *ton*." He smiled at her. "It is only when one has a family member who generates a never-ending stream of stories that one must worry unduly about one's reputation."

"Have you heard any more news of Lord Cambermere's exploits abroad?"

Lord William grimaced. "A letter two days ago, from a colleague in Rome. I shan't bother you with the salacious details, but suffice it to say that there is now at least one hotel in Italy that, in the future, will indeed be saying no to one particular duke." His chuckle was bitter and his eyes were grim.

Sarah's heart went out to him. For a man who valued propriety so highly, having a brother such as

Lord Cambermere had to be a heavy cross to bear. "Has he sent any word of his plans to return to England?"

"No. In fact, I have received only one missive from him since he left, asking me to hound a friend of his to repay some money he had borrowed." Lord William sighed. "George wouldn't think to notify me of something so mundane as his travel plans. I expect he and Harriet will just show up on my doorstep some evening."

"Harriet? Would she not be reluctant to appear in St. James's after dark?" The necessity of avoiding the masculine neighborhood had been impressed upon Sarah from almost the day she arrived in the capital, by everyone from Mrs. Templeton to the Cambermere tigers.

Lord William snorted. "Harriet is no stranger to the neighborhood after hours, believe me."

"Oh, yes, of course." Sarah could have bitten her tongue. Even a country miss such as she should know that actresses were not among the sheltered young women who could not risk a foray into St. James's. Embarrassed by the turn the conversation had taken, she shifted her gaze toward the embankment by the bridge—and promptly became even more embarrassed. There, half-hidden by the shadows cast by one of the stone arches, a young couple was enjoying an amorous embrace. The shadows revealed enough that Sarah felt a warm blush creeping up her neck.

Lord William, probably seeking the reason why she had stopped speaking, followed her gaze and frowned. "People should have more sense than to expose their private moments to public view," he muttered, running a finger beneath his neckcloth as he looked back at Sarah.

"Yes, yes, they should," she replied in a distracted voice. Why was she so taken aback by the encounter? True, it was unseemly for the young man and woman to be embracing in public, but the servants at Larkwood engaged in much the same behavior behind the barn or in the fields. She had even stumbled on a similar scene in the garden of a Chelsea town house several weeks ago while attempting to get some air during a long musicale hosted by one of Mrs. Templeton's friends.

All of this was true. Why, then, did accidentally coming upon *this* couple make Sarah so acutely uncomfortable?

She did not need to think long to find the answer. It was the company she was in, of course. Seeing the couple under the bridge brought all sorts of unwelcome thoughts to her mind.

The way she had felt when Lord William had lightly grazed her with Sam's short sword in the barn at Larkwood.

The sensation of sitting next to him in the carriage during the long trip to London.

The spark that had passed between them when he had kissed her hand at the end of the journey.

The sleepless night she had spent wondering if she had been a fool to refuse his offer of marriage.

Her cheeks became even more heated. Then she felt a fat drop of rain on her shoulder, followed by another.

"Perhaps we should return to the carriage," she said, her relieved voice coming out as a squeak. "It is a long journey back to Town."

He nodded, his own face red as he turned it up to the darkening sky. "You're right, perhaps we should."

In silence, they retraced their steps. When they came to the bend in the path, near the bridge, Sarah noted that the couple had vanished. Perhaps they, too, had sought protection from the rain, which was threatening to become a deluge any minute.

In the distance, she saw Lord Cambermere's tiger in the middle of the path, motioning them to hurry with one hand and pointing to the sky with the other.

"Shall we run?" asked Lord William. Without waiting for an answer, he grabbed her hand and pulled her along the path as an ominous roll of thunder sounded in the distance.

She hurried behind him. The raindrops were falling faster now, like tiny stones against her shoulders and hands. It wouldn't be the first time she'd been caught in the rain; in fact, getting wet in a storm rarely bothered her. But soaking her new gown and looking like a drowned rat in front of Lord William were things she wished to avoid if she could. He was moderating his pace to accommodate her shorter steps, she assumed, but it still took all her strength to keep up with him.

Suddenly, he yanked his hand from hers, stopped, and pulled off his jacket. He held it out to her.

"But Lord William, I—"

"For once in your life, could you not argue with me? I have a nice warm waistcoat, and a neckcloth and a shirt. All you have is that rather flimsy dress, and I already feel guilty enough without adding a case of galloping pneumonia to the list of ills my family has visited upon you."

His face brooked no argument, and she didn't want to slow down their return to the carriage. With a smile and a nod, she held her arms behind her and allowed him to pull his jacket over them. The moment he had finished, he seized her hand again and took off at a dead run.

Even as she tried to concentrate on not falling on the wet gravel or catching the hem of her skirt in her flying feet, Sarah spared a moment to appreciate the qualities of Lord William's coat. It was well tailored, certainly, and the fabric was fine. The buttons were polished to a high sheen. But her mind barely registered any of that. Mainly, it was warm and smelled of horses, and sandalwood, and soap.

Briefly, she closed her eyes against a new flood of impossible dreams, before opening her eyes again to follow Lord William across a small swath of slippery grass. The tiger had run ahead of them to pull back the carriage cover so they could scramble beneath. She pelted up the step just as a spear of lightning illuminated the riverside scene and the rain began to fall in earnest.

Laughing and gasping, she collapsed against the squabs of the curricle, deeply grateful that the tiger had protected the vehicle from the worst of the rain. Lord William leaped into the carriage as well and tossed his lithe frame onto the bench beside her. The tiger, already wearing a raincoat and carrying a vast umbrella obviously designed for a large man, let the leather cover fall and hopped up onto the back of the carriage.

Beneath the cover, the light was dim. It was like being in a very small tent, and it was rather more intimate than Sarah thought was wise. There was nothing for it, however, but to wait a few minutes and see whether the storm would pass. They would get soaked to the skin if they removed the cover and attempted to drive.

She looked down at her damp skirts and grinned. "Even when I try to dress like a lady, I inevitably end up looking the hoyden, do I not?" she asked breathlessly, turning to face Lord William.

When she saw the look on his face, a follow-up quip died on her lips. He was observing her as though he had just crossed a desert and she was a large, cold pitcher of ale.

"You look nothing like a hoyden, Lady Sarah," he said, his voice a husky rasp. Then, without warning, he lowered his head to hers and kissed her.

Being this close to him was like sitting next to him in the carriage on the way to London, except doubly, triply, immeasurably more so. She could focus on nothing but the feel of his lips on hers, warm and seeking. The sensation of his hands on her shoulders as he drew her close. The warmth of the raindrops that fell from his curling dark hair onto her neck.

It was like drowning in the sweetest honey. Sinking into the softest pillows. Curling up by the most welcoming fireside.

She raised her left hand to the back of his head and buried it deep in the damp hair at the base of his neck. Not until she felt the springy curls under her fingers did she realize she had wanted to do this since the moment she'd first set eyes on Lord William.

More tentatively, she raised one hand to his face and ran her fingertips along the stubble of his cheek. It felt like the finest sand. He gave a low moan and moved a hair's breadth away from her face.

"Do you have any idea what you do to me?" he murmured. His eyes were dark and heavy-lidded.

Slowly, she nodded. "If it is a mere fraction of the way you affect me, we are both in a great deal of trouble."

He grinned and drew her to him once more.

If his first kiss had been hungry, this one was cherishing. Slowly, he explored her lips with his, tasting and nibbling until she thought she would ignite with feelings she didn't even understand.

She dropped her hands to his shoulders, felt the taut muscles of his upper arms under the damp, light fabric. Wondered that she had ever, for a moment, considered him bookish. He had obviously been spending a great deal of time at Angelo's, she thought as she trailed her hands down his arms to his wrists.

Suddenly, he stopped his languorous exploration of her lips and wrenched himself away from her. He slid to the very edge of the bench and pinched the bridge of his nose.

Confused, she stared at him. Had she done something wrong?

Before she could ask, he spoke. "I am so sorry, Sarah. What must you think of me?" He closed his eyes, leaned his head against the top of the bench, and groaned.

What *did* she think of him? At the moment, she could think of nothing besides enticing him back to her.

But as the rising wind rattled the carriage cover and drew gooseflesh across her damp skin, she slowly returned to the real world, the one outside this tiny curricle. The world where people would insist that a man who had kissed a woman in such a way should seek to marry her. And the world where she could never do that, even if she wanted to. Despite what had just passed between them, she was not at all sure she would marry him, even if she could. She and the sober young lord were just too different.

She grasped his hand and squeezed. He opened his eyes and looked at her.

"I do not think one bit less of you, William," she said, dropping his title as he had dropped hers. It seemed foolish, really, to be formal with a man who had held her so intimately. "I played as much a role in what just happened as you did. If I had wished you to stop, I would have shouted for the tiger."

A slight smile touched the corner of his lips. Those wonderful lips. Sarah suppressed an urge to launch herself across the carriage again.

"I don't doubt that you would have." He chuckled. "But that does not change the fact that I should have exercised more self-control. If we all spent our lives giving in to every passing whim, we should not have much of a civilization."

"I don't know. I think civilization could use a bit more of what just passed between us," Sarah said tartly.

His laugh was deep this time. "Honestly, you are a true Original."

"I like to think so." She smiled back.

He paused. "But seriously, I had no right to initiate something neither of us can finish. You need a husband with more wealth than I shall ever know. And if I were ever to marry, I would need a wife who does not inspire me to reckless acts in public parks." His smile took some of the sting out of his words. Some, but not all.

"You appear to have thought all this out." She tried, and failed, to keep a note of childish bitterness out of her voice. He obviously viewed her as a serious threat to his precious decorum. That's what their interlude a few moments ago had been. A crack in his upright facade. No wonder he had pushed her away.

"Of course I've thought it all out," he replied, his tone maddeningly flat and reasonable. "That's what I do. Look at situations from all angles. Predict the best course of future action. It's what they teach us at Whitehall."

Silence fell between them. Sarah wondered if thoughts were plummeting through his brain in rapid, almost incomprehensible succession, as they were through hers.

If only they could—

If only her family had—

If only William was—

If only she—

If only—

If.

Utterly frustrated, she picked up her skirts and moved to the farthest corner of the bench, hoping that a bit of physical distance might help her to think more clearly. And, in a couple of moments, it did.

She looked down and realized she was still wearing William's jacket. She shifted in her seat and began to remove it.

"No, leave it, at least until we dry off a little." His voice was weary.

Nodding, she stopped her efforts and subsided against the seat. Then she came to a decision.

"We shall simply pretend this never happened," she announced. She came from a long line of people who were very, very good at ignoring reality. She would take a page from their book.

He shook his head. "We cannot. At least, *I* cannot."

She sighed as the import of his words sank in. "Neither can I. So I suppose we shall just have to determine how to live with it." The first solution that came to her mind had very little appeal, but lacking any other suggestions, she voiced it. "The first step, I suppose, is to avoid each other's company."

He lifted a corner of the carriage cover to peer out at the rain. "That would be prudent. And God knows, I am always prudent." A note of self-reproach underlay his words.

"In this case, restraint on both our parts may save us from further . . . entanglement." She thought how it had felt to tangle her fingers in his hair.

Stop it.

With a deep sigh, he turned away from his contemplation of the storm. The worst of the downpour appeared to be over. "You are right, of course," he said, turning to face her. He rested his elbows on his knees and steepled his fingers in front of his face. "I shall endeavor to stay out of your way, after tonight."

"Tonight?" Surely he was not still contemplating escorting her to the party?

William nodded. "I promised to introduce you to my friends. Whatever else I may be, I am not a man who breaks his promises."

"But William, I release you! Surely we cannot—"

"We can. I still do not think Henry Wolton worthy of a minute of your attention, let alone your hand in marriage." He frowned. "You must marry another, and the least I can do is attempt to find you a more respectable match than a half-crooked trader."

You must marry another. He was right, of course, and they both knew it.

Why, then, did the thought suddenly seem so new? And why did it hurt so much?

NINE

Sarah sat on the edge of the drawing room, speaking when spoken to and trying to act like a well-mannered guest.

When William had said that his friend was having a "small dinner party," she had assumed there would be perhaps a dozen guests. But when they had arrived at the enormous town house in Grosvenor Square, she had been astonished to see a huge table set for forty with glittering china and crystal.

"Well, perhaps Martindale's idea of 'small' is rather different than the rest of the world's," William had conceded when she'd reproached him quietly on their way in to dinner.

After the lavish meal, she had retired to the drawing room for tea and cakes with the ladies while the men indulged in port around the littered dining room table. But although she had managed some semblance of polite conversation with Mrs. Martindale, her hostess, and some of the other women, she felt dazed. She wondered if this was what it was like to walk in one's sleep.

Her thoughts drifted back to the carriage on the edge of Cholmondeley Walk. She continued to nod and add appropriate comments to the conversation, but she could still feel William's stubbled skin beneath her fingers. In fact, she could swear she could still sense his warm breath on her neck.

"Sarah? Are you all right?"

With a start, she realized she *had* felt his breath on her neck. He had bent low beside her so that he could whisper into her ear.

She glanced around, only realizing now that the gentlemen had rejoined the ladies. It appeared that she was not doing as good a job of participating in the party as she had thought.

"I am fine, thank you," she said, turning to smile at him. That was a mistake. His face was very close to hers.

She shrank back as though from a fire.

"I won't bite, you know," he said with an abashed grin. "I may ravish women in secluded carriages, but never have I been a rake in the middle of a crowded drawing room. Not prudent, you know." His smile did not quite reach his eyes, and she knew that he was still berating himself for giving into temptation this afternoon.

Despite his stiff-rumped attitude, despite his confidence that his answers were always right, she could not bear to see him punishing himself in this way. "And I limit my wantonness to areas outside the London city limits," she responded lightly, hoping to cheer him up. "So it seems rather unlikely that we shall cause a disturbance here in Mrs. Martindale's drawing room."

Her jest seemed to erase a little of the worry from his face, but he didn't reply. He merely extended his hand to escort her to the ballroom.

On their way down the corridor, her hand tucked securely in the crook of his elbow, he murmured, "I shall need to circulate among the crowd a bit, just so that no one gets the mistaken impression that we are a couple."

She felt herself bristle.

"That would make it more difficult for you to meet eligible gentlemen," he added.

Of course, she told herself. *You silly widgeon. Your purpose here is not to be with William. Your purpose here is to make wealthy acquaintances. Can you not remember the family debt for at least five minutes together?*

He scanned the corridor ahead of them. "I know that there are several men here who might be suitable. I noticed you conversing with Lord Goreham over dinner. Did you find him congenial?"

Not as congenial as another gentleman of my acquaintance. "Quite. He has quite an interest in botany." Interest was putting it mildly. *Obsession* might be closer to the truth. For over forty minutes, he had expounded on the propagation qualities of tea roses.

But at least he had all his own teeth.

"I'm glad you enjoyed talking to him. He is a bachelor, and staggeringly wealthy to boot. And he may not be as sensitive to *ton* gossip as some other men. Like me, he is blessed with rather . . . colorful siblings. In his case, two married sisters with a penchant for making fools of themselves over other women's husbands."

Sarah raised her eyebrows. She knew many society men and women turned a blind eye to their spouses' dalliances, so these sisters must have been quite indiscreet to attract attention.

"Not the usual affairs," William elaborated as they made slow progress, hemmed in by the rest of the crowd, toward the ballroom. "Edwina, the older, threatened suicide if the Marquess of Pedwell would not divorce his wife for her. Lord Pedwell ignored her, and she was forced to retract her threat because she had already transferred her affections to Francis Clarington. And the other sister, Georgiana—"

They reached the open double doors leading into the ballroom and entered, and whatever he had been about to say was drowned out by Sarah's gasp.

"What is it? What's wrong?" William asked.

She shook her head. "Nothing. But just *look* at this room!"

He scanned it. "I see nothing untoward. Does something unnerve you?"

"It is simply stunning."

None of the rooms in the houses she had visited with her cousin or Mr. Wolton had been half as opulent as this one. It was much more elaborate than was currently fashionable, but the Martindales had wisely—in Sarah's opinion—left all the gilded plasterwork and rococo flourishes in place. The ceiling was painted with some sort of mythological scene in rich hues of scarlet and peacock blue. Two enormous mirrors, one at each end of the room, reflected the light of hundreds of candles. On a dais at the far end of the room, a small ensemble was tuning its instruments.

William smiled. "I suppose I am a bit jaded. I've been coming to this house for years, and I'd forgotten the effect this room has on people who have never seen it before."

What must it be like, she wondered, to move so casually among people who had the blunt to maintain such luxury? Why, the coal bill alone for this town house must be substantial. She thought, fleetingly, of the east wing at Larkwood, closed years ago to save on heating costs. The roof already sagged badly, and the windows in the far bedroom leaked. She was certain there was dry rot in the conservatory, too. Not that it mattered. There hadn't been flowers in it since before Chadwick had been born.

Her family had once been able to move with pride in such circles. And they would again, if she could engage the interest of Lord Goreham. Or Mr. Wolton. Or anyone, really, who had money and who wasn't too particular. And if that rich gentleman could help her forget Lord William Cates, that would be a bonus.

Before she had a chance to ask William more about Lord Goreham's scandalous sisters, an older lady approached and laid a proprietary hand on William's arm.

"Lord William! I haven't seen you for ever so long!" she exclaimed. "I was just telling my friend Mrs. Ewart all about you—and here you are! I must introduce you to her—she has a friend who works in the foreign office, too!" Without so much as a glance at Sarah, the forceful lady began to march William across the room.

He cast an apologetic glance over his shoulder, and she smiled in return. He was not to blame for the older lady's rudeness, if rudeness it was. Sarah was fairly certain the dowager had not even noticed her.

William need not feel that he had to hover over her like a mother hen, in any case. She had been introduced to enough people at dinner that she could find someone to converse with. Glancing around, she spied Miss Amberley, a shy young woman who was attending the party with her rather formidable mother. Fortunately, the mother was nowhere in sight. Sarah strolled over to Miss Amberley's side.

"Are you enjoying the soiree?" she asked the younger woman.

"Very much," Miss Amberley replied. "I am glad the dancing is to start soon. I am very partial to dancing. Are you?"

Sarah shook her head. "I am not very skilled at it, but I do enjoy watching while others go through their paces."

They chatted for a few minutes about inconsequential matters, until Mrs. Amberley spied them.

"Charlotte, Lord Goreham was asking about you," Mrs. Amberley said, with a pointed look at Sarah. "I told him I would send you to him directly. I believe he is looking to add his name to your dance card."

Miss Amberley nodded. "Please excuse me," she said before hurrying across the room in the direction her mother pointed.

"Charlotte is a lovely girl, but she just needs a bit of direction now and then," Mrs. Amberley observed. "One must be so careful, as a mother, to ensure one's daughter has a successful season in

Town. It is so important to meet the right people, don't you agree?"

"Certainly," Sarah murmured, glancing about her to see if there was anyone else she knew whom she could draw into the conversation. No one. *Botheration.*

"Of course, you would know about that," Mrs. Amberley murmured. "You poor, poor girl."

Sarah suppressed a sigh. It had been at least a week since she had had to pick her way through a conversation like this, and she had fooled herself into believing that the firestorm over George's defection had finally abated.

But all of those conversations had taught her one thing: the key to deflecting the pity of condescending people was to refuse to be embarrassed by their innuendos. "There is no need to whisper, Mrs. Amberley," she said. "You are not discussing anything that has not already been dissected by every newspaper in London."

The older woman blinked. "You seem rather sanguine about the whole affair."

"What choice do I have?"

"You poor, poor girl," Mrs. Amberley said again, evidently hoping that a second declaration would cause Sarah to dissolve in a puddle of tears. "What humiliation, to be left at the altar!"

"Lord Cambermere hardly left me at the altar," Sarah remarked. "As I recall, he left me in Yorkshire."

"This is not a laughing matter, dear gel. Whatever will you do?"

As Mrs. Amberley continued what was clearly intended to be a monologue, Sarah let her thoughts

AN HONORABLE MATCH   167

drift once more. But instead of meandering back to the carriage in Richmond, they traveled further back, to William's offer of marriage.

She could not help but chide herself for assuming that his offer was based on pity. He had sworn at the time that it was based on honor and pragmatism, but she had not believed him. Her pride had convinced her that he pitied her.

It wasn't until she had reached London that she had realized what true pity was and how much it stung.

The opening bar of some sort of country dance echoed through the ballroom.

"I believe I am promised for this dance," Sarah lied, cutting off her companion in midsentence. "If you will excuse me." Hastily, she beat a retreat across the room. It had been cowardly to lie, but if she had had to listen to one more word of false sympathy, she would have been tempted to brandish her fan rather like a short sword and threaten Mrs. Amberley with a touché.

She was not promised for this dance, of course. She had successfully evaded the few invitations she had received. Her attendance at the soiree was designed to help her impress gentlemen, and none would be captivated by her flat-footed performance on the dance floor.

Scanning the room, she spotted a group of small gilt chairs in a dim corner. With luck, Mrs. Amberley had focused her attention on some other hapless victim and would not notice that Sarah was not among the dancers.

Settling herself on one of the chairs, she spread the full skirt of her evening dress about her. The dress was one of the few luxuries she had permitted herself when she spent the proceeds from the sale of the Cambermere emerald. She had not been able to resist the fine watered silk when the dress-maker had taken the bolt down from the wall. When Madame Saulnier had spread the shimmering fabric over a table, it had reminded Sarah of the brook that ran through the east pasture at Lark-wood. She had had it made up in a simple yet fashionable style, the sleeves a little wider and the neckline a little lower than what she was accustomed to wearing. Despite the slight extravagance, she was glad she had bought the dress. It made her feel confident, and she always needed an extra jolt of confidence after encounters with harridans like Mrs. Amberley.

Shaking off her lingering discomfort over the conversation, Sarah turned her attention to the dance floor. She had not lied when she had told the young Miss Amberley that she liked watching dancers. The complicated steps were fascinating. They reminded her of fencing moves.

In the middle of a long column of dancers she spotted William. He was looking sober and elegant tonight, flawlessly attired as always in a dark coat and buff pantaloons. It appeared that he, too, had eluded his elderly companion, for he was partnered with an elegant blond woman whom Sarah had not yet met.

They made their way through the pattern without stumbling once. The young woman laughed at something William said as he spun her back into place across from him.

Sarah suppressed a spurt of envy. She had no

right to be jealous of the unknown woman for attracting William's attention.

Tearing her gaze from William and his partner, she watched each top couple in turn make their way from the front of the line to the back with light, pretty steps. It did not look that difficult. If only she had a chance to learn, she was certain she could do it.

"Good evening, Lady Sarah," said Mrs. Martindale, taking a seat beside her. "Why aren't you dancing?"

"Perhaps I shall later," Sarah equivocated. "I wanted to simply enjoy the spectacle for a few moments first."

"Completely understandable, my dear. I'm so glad you could make it to our little party. Lord William has told us so much about you."

What on earth had he said? Sarah wondered. That she was a fortune-hunting fencer from the North of England with a half-mad family?

She dismissed that thought as quickly as it occurred to her. William had promised to do his best to smooth her way through London society, and she had no reason to doubt that he would keep his promise. It was only her own lingering doubts about her own worth that made her think such things.

"It was so kind of you to include me in the invitation," she told her hostess.

"It is so seldom that Lord William escorts anyone to our parties. When he asked if he could bring a guest, we were delighted."

"Oh, but Lord William and I are not—" She paused as she saw the gentleman himself approaching. Without her noticing, the music had ended, and the dancers were pausing to refresh themselves.

"A very talented ensemble," William told Mrs. Martindale. "They truly put us through our paces." And indeed it appeared they had, for his face was flushed.

"I am glad you enjoyed it," said their hostess as she stood and looked across the room. "I see my housekeeper signaling me—there must be some sort of crisis below stairs." With a gay little wave, she departed.

William took the seat she had vacated. "What are you doing, sitting over here alone?" he asked, frowning. "I was watching you from the dance floor."

Briefly, she told him how she'd escaped from Mrs. Amberley.

"She's a most unpleasant woman—I don't know why the Martindales continue to invite her. Unless, of course, it's the fact that her brother is one of our superiors at the foreign office." He smiled. "But I have one way to keep you out of her way. Join me for a dance."

Sarah shook her head. "I believe I mentioned that I have no skill on the dance floor." Yet another city talent she had not mastered. Surely he must think her a complete rustic.

"But you have natural grace. I'm sure I can teach you."

She laughed. "Unless there is an opportunity to parry and riposte out there, I suspect my 'grace' will be of little use. The patterns of the steps are complicated."

He shrugged. "So we'll waltz, then."

She felt her eyes widen. "I did not think that dance was acceptable in Society."

He plucked a loose thread from his sleeve, and she found herself wondering if she had similar loose threads hanging from her garment. It had never occurred to her to check.

"Perhaps waltzing is forbidden in the rarefied precincts of Almack's, but not everyone in London is quite so hidebound," William said. "Most of the people here are affiliated in some way with the diplomatic service and have spent time abroad. In Vienna, children learn to waltz practically from the moment they learn to walk. We think nothing of it."

"Oh." For a moment, Sarah could not think of a suitable response. And then, "But I don't know the steps to that, either."

"It's simple. I'll teach you on the dance floor."

"But—"

He reached for her hand, held it, and squeezed it, and she forgot the argument she had been about to make.

"You can't simply sit here all night talking to our hostess and pushy matrons and shy young girls. I brought you here to meet gentlemen." He scanned the crowd.

"And how is dancing with you going to help me accomplish that end?" she asked. "Aren't we trying to convince everyone that we are not here together?"

He returned his attention to her. "Well, you do have a point. Except that sitting here in the corner watching the proceedings isn't useful either. At least dancing will show you off to the company."

"Rather like a horse at Tattersall's? Will they want to check my teeth, too?"

William blew out a puff of air. "Be childish if you like. This husband hunt is your idea, not mine. If you do not want my help, just say so."

A wave of contrition washed through Sarah. She hung her head as she realized how ridiculously she was behaving. She squeezed his hand as he had squeezed hers, then released it. "You're right, William. I *am* being childish. If you dare to take me out on the dance floor with no prior instruction, then by all means, I am at your disposal and in your debt."

He rose, executed a neat little bow, and held out his hand. "Your servant, m'lady."

She stood as well. "How shall we know when the dance is a waltz?"

He raised one eyebrow. "You really don't know much about dancing, do you?"

"I told you as much."

He held up a hand. "Don't worry. I believe you. Listen to the rhythm of the music. When you hear the opening bars of a piece that sounds different from all the others, that will be the waltz. I believe one is coming up on the program next."

And indeed, within a moment the ensemble began playing a piece with a strange, wild, lilting rhythm. Sarah had long wondered why people felt the need to dance. She enjoyed music, but she didn't seem to have the compulsion to caper to it that so many others did. But this music seemed made for movement.

She allowed William to lead her onto the dance

floor. As he raised one hand and indicated that she should do the same, she grinned.

"It's not too late, you know. You can still turn back, while there's time to save your feet."

He grinned in return. "It's not my feet I'm worried about." And with that cryptic comment, he took her raised hand in his. "Now put your other hand on my shoulder."

She did as he instructed, ignoring the fact that her fingers were now dangerously close to the nape of his neck. When he slid a hand around her waist, she jumped.

"This is how the dance is done," he murmured.

She looked around at the other dancers, saw that he told the truth, and relaxed a little. Biting her lip, she nodded. This dance looked like it would require coordination and previous skill, no matter what he said.

"Now, I know you will find this difficult, but just follow my lead."

"What do you mean?"

He laughed. "Just do as I do. If I try to turn us to the left, just let me do it. If my feet move one way, guide your feet the same way."

She nodded. "That sounds straightforward."

"It is. Here we go." And with no more notice than that, they were off, joining a throng of other spinning dancers circling the floor.

Within two revolutions, Sarah had managed to step on the hem of her dress. She pitched slightly forward, but William braced himself and steadied her.

"That's all right," he encouraged her. "Everyone stumbles in their first few times out. Just keep going." His hand strong on the small of her back, he spun her in an elegant circle. "If it helps, count the beats in your head. One-two-three, one-two-three."

"One-two-three," Sarah echoed, although to be truthful, she could not concentrate on much else besides the dangerous thrill of being in his arms again. Although they were in the middle of a crowded party, surrounded by other dancers, his breath against her ear as they spun around the polished floor was almost her undoing. His unique scent—a combination of spices and soap and something indefinable—enveloped her.

The room spun by crazily as she struggled to keep up with his long, fluid steps. Faces known and unknown swept across her field of vision. Candles shimmered in some hazy distance. And still she and William spun. She felt as though she were flying.

"Are you enjoying it?" he asked.

She nodded, although *enjoy* seemed such a pallid word for the emotions coursing through her. She not only felt graceful. For the first time in two years, she felt *free*. Free of her obligations, free of worry, free of guilt. Just flying, free as a bird.

The dance ended all too soon. The ensemble put down their instruments and the assembled dancers applauded. William released her and stepped back. She drew in a deep breath of air, hoping to clear her head.

It was maddening, really, how unaffected he appeared to be by their contact. Except for that one mad moment in the carriage this afternoon, he always seemed cool, urbane, and in control. Bearing with such personal rigor, day in and day out, would surely become wearing after a while.

No matter how pleasant a package that rigor was wrapped in.

"You are a very good dancing instructor," she said, dropping him a brief curtsey.

"I have had a lot of practice. Social events are always a large part of any diplomatic conclave, and I have spent many nights dancing with diplomats' wives who could benefit from a bit of extra dance instruction."

Soon he would be back in his world of international negotiations and social events, she thought as they left the dance floor. It was a world she had neither the skills nor the desire to enter. After just a few weeks of social events in London, she was completely exhausted. Living that sort of life all the time, and moving from place to place as well, would be akin to purgatory.

"Cates!" a voice called out behind them. They turned to see a tall blond man approaching.

"Finworth!" William replied with evident delight. "I didn't know you were here."

"I had a previous engagement, so I was not able to attend the dinner. I just arrived a few minutes ago." The two men shook hands, then William turned to Sarah.

"Fin, I'd like to introduce you to Lady Sarah Harrison. Lady Sarah, this is Gerald Linton, Lord Finworth. If I remember correctly, the Marquess of Finworth, Earl Greywood, and Viscount Littlefield."

The blond man laughed. "Don't forget Prince of Pedantry and Duke of Brandy. We were at Oxford together," Lord Finworth explained to Sarah. "Wills knows all my faults."

"And virtues, too," William inserted, with an almost imperceptible nod at Sarah. "So any major upheavals in your life since last we met, Fin? Are you married, in trouble with the law, famous?"

"None of the above. Still single, blameless, and unknown." The blond man grinned.

"So are you in the diplomatic service as well?" Sarah asked.

Lord Finworth laughed. "Good God, no! I hate to travel. No, I'm a boring old farmer from Shropshire. I have several estates and spend most of my time in the country. London is more than exotic enough for my tastes."

William raised his eyebrows and smiled. Really, for a diplomat, the man was obvious. He might well throw her and Lord Finworth in a room together, lock the door and declare her compromised, forcing his friend to the altar, she thought.

But she had to admit he had done what he had promised. Lord Finworth was young, charming, and unmarried. And if William's speaking glances were any indication, he was likely rich as well.

"Do you come often to London, Lady Sarah? I am quite sure I have never seen you before."

She shook her head. "No, this is my first time. I'm afraid I am a bit of a country mouse, Lord Finworth."

"We are mice of the same fur, then," he said. "I see, however, that you like to dance. May I reserve the honor of the next waltz?"

"You may, indeed," she said, hope fluttering in her chest. Perhaps the friendly Lord Finworth

would engage her affections more than the stolid
Mr. Wolton had so far. And maybe, just maybe, he
would help her forget her exasperating fascination
for William Cates.

Why didn't I think of Fin sooner? William wondered
as he watched Sarah and his old school friend spinning around the dance floor. Well, perhaps
"spinning" was too positive a word. Fin wasn't much
better at waltzing than Sarah was, so they made a
few stops and starts and once narrowly avoided
crashing into Goreham and his partner.

But truly, Fin was perfect for Sarah. He was rich,
he was kind, and he rarely came to Town, so he
probably wouldn't give two hoots about the jilting
scandal, which was beginning to ebb in any case.
And William had known Fin was in London—he'd
run into him several weeks ago in White's.

So why hadn't he introduced him to Sarah long
before now?

William returned his attention to the dance floor.
Sarah was looking down at her feet as Fin said
something to her. She looked up again, and as they
executed a fairly competent turn, she gave him a
brilliant smile.

Something deep and primal twisted in William's
gut, and he knew that the reason he hadn't introduced her to Fin was that he'd *known* they would
find each other congenial. Ridiculous as it was, he
wanted to keep her all to himself.

Be reasonable, he told himself as he turned away
from the dance floor and wandered into the corridor. *She needs a fortune and you have none. A wife*

*would be nothing but an expensive inconvenience in your
line of work. She has none of the attributes of a perfect
diplomat's wife: She can't dance, she's awkward in
crowds, and she doesn't have tame, common hobbies that
she can discuss easily with the other diplomats' wives. She
fences, for heaven's sake.*

He ran a hand through his hair as he continued
down the corridor. All of these things were true.
Why, then, had he behaved like a cow-eyed schoolboy in the carriage in Richmond?

It had just seemed the most natural thing in the
world, to kiss her. She'd looked so appealing—
flushed from their dash through the rain, with one
long chestnut curl loose from her harum-scarum
coiffeur and trailing across her cheek. And seeing
that couple under the bridge had put all sorts of
unrealistic thoughts in his head.

Unrealistic, indeed, he thought as he wandered
down the staircase, barely acknowledging the greet-
ings of fellow guests as his mind continued to race.
At the door, he eschewed the butler's offer of his
hat and coat. "I shall be returning in a moment,"
he said, and opened the front door.

The night air was blessedly cool. The rain earlier
in the day had dispersed the heat, and the night
was now cloudless. A few stars sparkled down on
Mayfair as he inhaled great drafts of fresh air. It was
odd—he spent much of his social life in gatherings
such as this one, but never before had he found
one as confining.

Perhaps because never before had he attended a
party with Sarah and watched her laughing as she
danced in the arms of another man.

Damn it all, he had fallen in love with the last woman in England who would have him.

He'd known it, of course, and not only today in the carriage. He'd known it when he'd realized that she wasn't hunting a fortune for money's sake, but solely to save her family. He'd known it when she'd explained her mother's odd clothing with such empathy. Hell, he'd probably known it from the moment she'd brandished a sword in his direction and dared him to fence with her.

But knowing that he loved her changed nothing. She would never veer from her determination to save her family. And as he had told her, he could never countenance a life of indolence in London, living on his income and contributing nothing to the greater world. Diplomacy was his lifeblood, the reason he got out of bed in the morning. Forced to give it up, he would be bitter. And forced to participate in it, Sarah would be miserable.

There was no help for it, William thought, sighing in disgust and turning to reenter the town house. He would have to ensure that Sarah married another, and the sooner the better.

She was already well on her way, he thought as he opened the door and crossed the foyer once more. Fin and Goreham both seemed interested, and even Wolton—scapegrace that he was—could provide the funds Sarah so desperately needed. Surely one of them would soon recognize her worth, her utter uniqueness, and step forward to solve her dilemma.

The time had come, William realized, for him to step back and leave her to finish her task alone. By hanging about, he would simply distract her. It wasn't self-flattery to realize that she had been as passionate in the carriage as he had. She might not love him—likely she did not—but she was certainly drawn to him. And that attraction would do her no good as she tried to find a more suitable husband.

As he climbed the stairs, he resigned himself to the fact that this might be the last time he would see Lady Sarah Harrison until she was safely betrothed to another. Although he was safe in warm, dry London, he felt as though he was back on the gray, wet Yorkshire moors as he trudged back along the corridor and rejoined the festivities.

TEN

The gossipmongers really did appear to have moved on to fresher scandals, Sarah thought with relief as she perused the morning papers.

Mrs. Templeton adored the papers and subscribed to almost all of them. She preferred to read them with her breakfast, and Sarah had adopted the habit. It was intriguing to learn about the continuing efforts to negotiate a settlement with France.

Reading the newspaper was the only way she *would* learn anything about the peace negotiations, Sarah thought as she popped a thick morsel of ham into her mouth. She certainly couldn't ask William for details, as he had barely spoken to her since the Martindales' party a month ago. As she had known he would, he had adhered to his promise to stay away from her. He had called twice, stayed for a proper ten minutes each time, and spoken of nothing but unremarkable things. Both times, her mother and cousin had been in the room. It had all been most decorous, which was only right. And it was no surprise. As William himself had said, he was nothing if not prudent.

What had she ever found appealing in such a stiff-rumped man?

He isn't always stiff-rumped, a tiny voice reminded her. *On the rare occasions when he stops trying to be perfect, he is far from prim.*

Those occasions *were* rare, however. Living under the constant threat of his disapprobation would be wearing, she thought for the thousandth time. Despite the fact that he was undoubtedly an accomplished kisser, she and he would never suit.

Sighing, Sarah returned her attention to the gossip columns. Fortunately, there was not a word about Lord Cambermere returning to London; Sarah checked faithfully for such rumors every day. It appeared that the duke and his new wife planned to stay in Italy until the Season was over, and that suited Sarah very well.

The column in her hand included only some innuendo about a Lady S——, who had apparently been seen in the company of a Mr. Y—— in Brighton, when everyone had been led to believe she was at a country house party in Oxfordshire. And a Lord B—— was being taken to task for profligate spending. Well, Sarah could empathize with the hapless Lord B——. Only yesterday, she had received a desperate letter from her father.

We've had to sell Daisy, he had written, and Sarah's heart had jumped into her throat. Daisy was Hester's favorite horse. Her sister would be devastated. Sarah understood her father's decision; the other horses were workhorses and could be used to improve the estate's fortunes. But Daisy had been strictly a riding horse, and she was a luxury the Harrisons could no longer afford. If her father had been forced to sell Daisy, the situation had to be grim indeed. Time was running out if her marriage idea was to succeed at all.

"What are your plans for the day, my dear?" Mrs. Templeton piped up from the other side of the table, where she was half-hidden behind a copy of the *Morning Post*. They were alone in the breakfast room, Mr. Templeton having long ago left for his shop and Lady Glenmont still in bed. Sarah's mother had taken to Town hours with great gusto and rarely rose before noon.

"Mr. Wolton is taking me for a drive in Hyde Park," Sarah said, trying to summon up some enthusiasm for the outing.

"Along with our excursion to the theater this evening?" Her cousin lowered the newspaper. "It sounds as though he is finally becoming serious about his suit."

"Do you think so?" Sarah both hoped and dreaded that that was true.

Mrs. Templeton nodded. "Perhaps he has had wind of your other beaux and decided that he needs to move quickly, before someone else does."

Sarah's laugh was bitter. "He has nothing to fear from that quarter."

Mrs. Templeton raised her eyebrows. "But what about Lord Goreham?"

"He has left London on an extended trip to Scotland and does not plan to return until later this year. We said our farewells the night he escorted me to Vauxhall."

"Why did you not mention this to me sooner?"

Sarah sighed. "I suppose because I was so mortified that yet another gentleman had found me wanting."

Her cousin clucked her tongue. "Nonsense, Sarah. Just because a few blind bucks cannot recognize a true diamond when they see one is no reason to feel unworthy."

Sarah smiled. Mrs. Templeton and her mother had been her most stalwart supporters over the last two months.

"Well, there's always Lord Finworth. He is very charming."

"Yes, he is." Sarah repressed a sigh. Lord Finworth had truly been the most promising of all her suitors—all the ones with plump purses, that is. After the Martindales' party, he had escorted Sarah on several occasions, including an evening at the theater and an outing to Kew Gardens. They had enjoyed each other's company quite well—in fact, she considered him a very good friend. She would have been more than happy to receive an offer from him, but he had confided that he hoped to marry for love, and that while he liked her very much, well—

She had assured him she understood. His wealth gave him the luxury of choosing a wife who was more than a mere partner.

Yesterday, when Mrs. Martindale had come to Paradise Row to pay a call, she had revealed that Lord Finworth had tumbled "head over heels" for a young woman named Miss Elizabeth Danes. According to another friend, he had already sent her several extravagant bouquets. "Roses *and* orchids, my dear!" Mrs. Martindale had exclaimed. "Every day, for a week! The gentleman is smitten, I'm afraid."

"I don't think I shall be able to wrest Lord Finworth's attentions away from Miss Danes," Sarah told her cousin now.

"Oh, Mrs. Martindale was just telling tales!" Mrs. Templeton extracted a lump of sugar from the silver cup on the table and stirred it into her tea.

"I don't believe she was. Have you not noticed that Lord Finworth has not paid us a call in more than a week?"

Mrs. Templeton stopped stirring, lifted the cup to her lips, and sipped before replying. "Well, he might be busy."

Sarah smiled. "Thank you for your optimism, but I need to be realistic. I believe I must pin all my hopes on Mr. Wolton."

Mrs. Templeton's mouth drew down in a small moue of distaste. "The more I see of Mr. Wolton, the less I favor him. I cannot imagine why Thomas even sent such a gentleman our way."

"Mr. Templeton was thinking very astutely," Sarah replied, wiping her mouth with her napkin. "Mr. Wolton is just seedy enough to need the respectability of an old family name and just rich enough to suit my purposes. He seems to be waiting for something, though. I wish he would come to a decision. There are only a few weeks left in the Season, and I must move quickly."

Mrs. Templeton reached across the table and squeezed her hand. "You know that, whatever happens, you and Margaret—along with the rest of your family—are most welcome to stay with Thomas and me for as long as you wish."

Tears pricked at the back of Sarah's eyes. Mrs. Templeton was so very kind. But there was no conceivable way that she would be able to shelter the entire Harrison clan in her little house. "Thank you, Mrs. Templeton, but—"

Her cousin squeezed her hand again. "Don't dismiss the offer out of hand. I know we don't have a great deal of room here, but we would manage. I would rather see that than see you without a proper home."

Without a proper home. The words strengthened Sarah's resolve. "It will not come to that," she said firmly. "I have an odd feeling that Mr. Wolton may just be about to come to the rescue of us all."

With that statement, she picked up her newspaper again, hoping that her cousin would take the hint that the discussion was at an end. Thankfully, she did, and silence descended on the little table once more.

But instead of concentrating on the journal, Sarah found her thoughts drifting back to Mr. Wolton. If she was reading the situation correctly, she suspected that he would make his offer before the week was out. He had made a cryptic reference to Rundell, Bridge & Rundell last week, and she had later learned that the shop was one of London's finest jewelers. The scandal had finally died down, and the Season was about to close. Mr. Wolton knew those facts as well as Sarah did.

Within the week, Sarah could find herself betrothed for the second time this year. And this time, she wouldn't allow anything to interfere with her plans. She'd ask him to get a special license so that they could be married immediately, if she had to.

Married immediately, to Mr. Wolton. Her stomach churned at the thought. He was good-looking and rich. His manners were adequate. He could even maintain an entertaining conversation. Certainly, he had a few shady dealings in his past—a few discreet questions to some of Mr. Templeton's friends had confirmed what William had told her—but it was not as though she could claim that her family was lily-white when it came to financial management. All those creditors *had* expected to be paid, after all.

No, a betrothal to Mr. Wolton—if, indeed, he was planning to offer for her—would be the answer to all her family's prayers. She would just have to stifle her childish disappointment in the fact that her heart didn't leap when she saw him and her mind did not race with improper ideas about him as she lay wakeful in her bed at night.

Such things were for women with choices, Sarah told herself. She had none, and she should be grateful that salvation was at hand.

So why did she feel so ill?

Lightheadedness, she decided. She needed to eat a bit more, settle her nerves. She stood and crossed the room to the sideboard. There were few vicissitudes in life, she concluded, that could not be mitigated by a piece of toast with jam.

"The park seems somewhat quieter than usual today," Sarah said as Mr. Wolton slapped the reins smartly and the horse picked up speed.

"It could be the weather," he said. It was, indeed, rather cool for July, and there was a chilly breeze.

"But I think that many of the *ton* are heading off to the country. Within a few weeks, London will be as deserted as Dartmoor." He smiled. "Not that that is a disadvantage. Gives those of us who remain here all year room to move."

Remain here all year. She'd been trying not to think about that part of any agreement she might come to with Mr. Wolton. To be trapped in this huge, loud, dirty city all the time, never to see open fields or free-roaming animals unless she could convince someone to undertake an excursion to the country. Of course, she would be able to visit her family at Larkwood. But that was a long journey, and she could not foresee making it very often.

She smiled brightly at her companion. "I am curious to see the city when things are quieter."

"In the winter, if the Thames freezes, I shall take you to the Frost Fair."

The winter. That sounded like long-term planning. Perhaps she really had read the winds correctly, and Mr. Wolton was about to make his offer. She offered up a silent prayer that he would do so soon, for her family's sake.

"That sounds lovely." Sarah tried to make her voice sound encouraging. She was so close to achieving her goal that she could barely speak for fear of ruining everything. "I would love to see London in the winter." It was frightening, really, how skilled she had become at lying.

Mr. Wolton smiled. "That is good. I was concerned that you might find it dreary."

"Not at all. Especially if I knew I would have the pleasure of your company."

His smile widened. "Lady Sarah, there is something I would like to ask you—"

Sarah held her breath.

"—tonight, after the theater. You do not have another engagement this evening, do you?"

She exhaled slightly and shook her head. "No. I would be happy to spend time with you after the performance."

His grin became even wider. "Excellent! I am picking up a package early this evening—at one of the city's finest shops—and I wanted to have it in hand before speaking with you."

He could not have been much more obvious if he had taken out an ad in the *Times*, she thought. He must be going back to Rundell, Bridge & Rundell to collect the ring. His eagerness to imply the costliness of the gift was somewhat improper, but she had to keep reminding herself that his fortune was newly minted and he wasn't as skilled in dealing with it as were gentlemen who had been wealthy for generations.

Relief, sweet and heady, rushed over her. By the end of the night, all this performing and worrying would be finished. And if that meant that she had to marry a man she did not love and spend her life in a city she did not like, those were very small prices to pay.

"Lovely, Mr. Wolton. I shall look forward to it."

"No, Sally, you take the seat at the front, where you will be better able to see the play," Lady Glenmont said, settling into a chair at the rear of the box Mr. Wolton had secured for their outing.

"If you're certain, Mother," Sarah replied.

"Of course, dear. I've had many chances to attend the theater. Besides, it would be far too awkward for me to maneuver into one of those seats. I am just as happy back here, where I can comment on all the action to Mr. and Mrs. Templeton."

"Thank you," Sarah replied with a rush of gratitude for her parent. She was more excited to be attending the theater than she cared to admit. Even though she had seen a number of performances since their arrival in London, she still felt a small thrill every time she had the opportunity to see a play. This would be one advantage of remaining in London, she consoled herself—she would be able to attend the theater every night there was a performance, if she so wished.

As they took their seats, she heard a few murmurings from neighboring boxes and saw several covert glances cast their way. It was nothing she had not become accustomed to, and she resolved to ignore them. After all, if she wasn't mistaken, she would soon be betrothed to Mr. Wolton and safe from the derision of the *ton*.

Mr. Wolton was turned around in his chair to reply to something Mr. Templeton had said, and Sarah studied his profile. He was certainly a handsome man, and he had treated her with great courtesy during the weeks of their acquaintance. He had made it clear that he did not love her, just as she did not love him, but they were both pursuing an alliance with other goals in mind and had been perfectly honest about that.

She doubted whether she could ever love him,

but she was fairly certain that they could have an amiable life together. Soon, perhaps, there would even be children to occupy her days. It would not be an exciting life, but it would be a secure one— for her and for her family. It seemed certain he was about to make an offer any day now, and she should be glad.

Sarah turned her attention to the crowd that was filling the theatre. It looked as though there would hardly be an empty seat in the house—not surprisingly, as this play had generated a lot of attention in the press. The actor playing the lead role was being hailed as a worthy rival of the other current hero of the theater scene, Edmund Kean.

A commotion in the stalls near the door caught her attention. Someone had shouted above the general hum of the crowd, and several people were looking about wildly. A man shaded his eyes against the glare of the massive chandelier dangling from the ceiling and pointed toward a box on the far side of the theater.

"There she is!"

Who had arrived? Sarah craned her neck to get a better look. Perhaps it was the Czar's sister, or even Queen Caroline. Her appearance at the Opera recently had caused quite a stir.

A beautiful blond woman dressed in a peacock blue dress had just entered the box that seemed to be the focus of the crowd's attention. She wore an enormous necklace of what looked from this distance to be sapphires, and similarly large drops dangled from her ears. Her wrists were laden with so many bracelets that Sarah wondered whether the lady could actually lift her arms.

Who on earth was she? She looked vaguely familiar, but Sarah was certain they had never met before.

"Your Grace!" bellowed someone from the stalls.

"All hail the Duchess of Drury Lane!" came a cry from one of the balconies.

The Duchess of Drury Lane. The glittering blond woman was the actress with whom Lord Cambermere had fled the country. Sarah felt cold beads of sweat breaking out on her forehead, and her palms were instantly damp. Moments later, her one-time fiancé entered the box behind his wife and took his seat.

"It's the Jilting Duke!" rose another shout, crystal clear above the tumult.

Sarah's mind raced. When had the duke and duchess come to Town? She had heard not a word. Why hadn't Lord William warned her?

"Good Lord," Mr. Wolton muttered. "He's actually had the nerve to bring his doxy out in public."

The Cambermeres leaned toward the edge of their box and smiled with what looked like delight as a low, ominous hooting rose from the stalls below. At first, it was hard to distinguish the words, but a few chants soon became clear. "Duchess, duchess, blond and luscious," went one of the less scurrilous ones.

She watched in horrified fascination as the new Lady Cambermere gave her tormentors a gleeful wave. So absorbed was Sarah in the duchess's performance that she was unaware of anything else in the theater until she heard a sound emanate from Mr. Wolton that could only be termed a growl. She glanced at him with concern. "Are you all right, sir?"

He shook his head and nodded to the stalls below. When Sarah followed his glance, her stomach felt as it had once when she had tripped and fallen over a stile as a child. More and more faces in the crowd had shifted their focus from the Cambermere box to the one occupied by Sarah's own party. Many of those faces wore mocking grins.

A voice rose up from the floor. "Lady Sarah! If you can sit there stone-faced, you're a better actress than Harriet Partridge ever was!"

Sarah's shame receded, to be replaced by scorching, blinding anger. She was tired of being the object of strangers' derision. As she had complained to her cousin so many times, *she* had done nothing wrong.

"Don't even say Lady Sarah's name, you filthy beggars!" Mr. Wolton roared, rising from his chair to shake his fist at the crowd. His face was mottled and his eyes were lit with a strange fire she had never seen in them before.

Sarah shrank back in her seat in appalled disbelief. This was rapidly escalating into a scene far worse than her wildest nightmares.

"Those who sit with lady beggars shouldn't throw stones!" shouted a woman in a bright yellow gown. "Begging for pennies or a fortune, 'tis all the same thing."

Sarah's breath was coming in short, sharp gasps. She had to run, she had to hide, she had to leave, she had to go home to Yorkshire. She couldn't do this any more.

"Who said that?" Mr. Wolton thundered, leaning

over the railing and shaking his cane at the crowd. "I shall call you out, sir! I shall call you out!"

Sarah tugged at Mr. Wolton's sleeve. The fact that he had just called a woman "sir" would only encourage the mob to throw out further insults. She had to calm him. If he would simply stay quiet, the furor would blow over.

"Mr. Wolton, please, sit down. They will soon lose interest in us if you do not egg them on."

Wild-eyed, he looked at her. It took a moment or two before he appeared to focus on her and realize who she was.

"Scoundrels," he muttered. Then he turned his attention back to the railing. "Scoundrels!" he bellowed.

Laughter rippled through the crowd.

Sarah looked toward the back of the box to see her mother and the Templetons frozen in horror. There would be no help from that quarter. If anyone was going to put an end to this disaster, it was going to be her.

It galled her to give the crowd the satisfaction of driving her from the theater, but that would likely be the only way to quell the firestorm. Deliberately, she stood and plucked Mr. Wolton's jacket once more.

"Please, let us go. I shan't enjoy the performance, and I don't believe you will either. They won't stop howling until they have nothing left to howl at."

"Good for you, Lady Sarah!" shouted someone. "Run back to Yorkshire!"

If she had had the strength, she would have done exactly that.

"Stop pulling at me, woman," Mr. Wolton muttered. "Just give me time, and I'll make them be quiet."

He was not the only one concerned with calming the crowd. Far below on the stage, a man in a dun-colored jacket walked from the wings and tried to catch the mob's attention.

"Ladies and gentlemen." His querulous, high-pitched shouts were barely audible. "The performance is about to begin! Please take your seats! Please take your seats!"

He might as well have been trying to bring a pack of rabid dogs to heel. If anything, his entreaties seemed to spur the crowd on to more outrageous comments.

"I challenge you to come up here and repeat that!" Mr. Wolton cried as he waved his fist at an unseen heckler.

She glanced over at the duke's box, hoping to catch Lord Cambermere's eye and convince him, somehow, to quit the building. If he and his duchess were gone, perhaps that would quiet the crowd. But instead of the duke, her eye was drawn to another figure who was just entering the box, his hat still in his hand. William.

She watched as he appeared to take in the nature of the spectacle in a moment or two. He leaned over his brother's chair and spoke into his ear. The duke replied, and Lord William looked up and directly at the box where Sarah sat. Even from this distance, she could sense that he was trying to bolster her spirits, simply through his gaze. And oddly enough, she did find it bracing.

The noise in the theater had risen to such a pitch that it had long since swallowed the theater manager's pitiful cries. William pushed past his brother and stood at the edge of the Cambermere box.

"The show here is done," she heard his voice echo above the crowd. Several faces in the stalls swiveled to stare at him. A few people pointed.

"Turn your attention to the stage. That is the show you have come to see." Lord William's face was like a thundercloud, and his voice rang with authority. There was little he could do if they did not comply, but by his voice and his manner he implied that he was deadly serious. If she had been one of the rabble-rousers, she would have thought twice about shouting out another insult.

Was he doing this to save his family's precious honor, she wondered, or to help her save face? She did not know, and she did not care. All that mattered was whether it worked.

"Do you want to waste the money you have spent to attend the performance?" William asked the rabble. "The cast is likely to be in fine form tonight."

Good Lord, he was *reasoning* with them. Sarah's astonishment grew when she realized his tactic was working. Already, the crowd seemed somewhat quieter.

"What does money mean to me?" bellowed a belligerent voice from one of the other stalls. Sarah twisted her head to see who had spoken and recognized the Marquess of Dinsmore, one of wealthiest members of the *ton*.

"It may not mean anything to you, but not all of us are so lucky," Lord William shot back without missing a beat. "If you had any sense of noblesse oblige, you would be quiet and allow others less fortunate than you to enjoy the performance."

Sarah's smile was so wide she thought her face would crack. Lord William's skills as a diplomat were on show for all of London to see. How much more effective they were than Mr. Wolton's childish taunts!

Lord Dinsmore frowned but settled back in his seat. He said something to Lady Dinsmore but did not favor the theater with any further public comments.

The people in the stalls had begun to calm down as well, perhaps distracted by the antics of an acrobat, who had taken the stage the moment the noise began to fade. It appeared that they had become bored of the drama of Lady Sarah and the Cambermeres, at least for the moment.

But what of tomorrow? Sarah was sure that the newspapers for the rest of the week would be full of news of this spectacle. All the columnists who had taken such glee in Lord Cambermere's elopement would be eager to write about this latest development.

She sighed. At least she would not need to worry this time. Her betrothal to Mr. Wolton was all but assured. And even though that thought was filling her daily with less and less pleasure, the fact remained that her family would be safe. With that in mind, she could bear any disaster. What harm could the barbed tongues of the press and the *ton* do her now?

Before turning her attention to the stage, she spared a glance at the Cambermere box. William caught her eye and flashed her a brilliant smile. It so reminded her of the first time she had seen him grin, in the barn at Larkwood as they fenced, that her breath caught in her throat. How could a man so stiff-rumped look so rakish?

She smiled back at him, hoping she could convey without words the depth of her gratitude for his intervention. And as she smiled, a realization struck her so forcefully that her heart started to hammer. Lord William Cates was a man one could rely on. And Mr. Wolton, for all his blunt, was not. He had neither Lord William's confidence nor his sense of honor. And he had never once made her feel as she felt right now, as she watched William gracefully sink into his seat and shift his gaze to the performance below. He steepled his fingers and rested his chin on them, in a gesture that was so familiar and, suddenly, so endearing.

When she married Mr. Wolton, it was possible that she would rarely see William. They would move in very different social circles. A band of panic tightened around her chest. And as she continued to review her situation, she felt tears prickling at the backs of her eyes.

Why did she have to marry a fortune?

Don't be ridiculous, she told herself, blinking rapidly and twisting her head back toward the performers. *You have come all the way to London to find a rich husband. And, with luck, you soon will. You cannot allow yourself to be diverted from your goal by a gentleman who cannot serve that purpose.*

And that goal was growing more important by the day. She thought of the letter from her father. He had sold Daisy to pay the debt he had incurred six years ago to repair the Larkwood roof. Those men knew the glaziers who had fixed the window in the drawing room three years ago, and they would no doubt tell their friends that a few well-placed threats would induce Lord Glenmont to pay his debts.

If she did not succeed in bringing Mr. Wolton to the point soon, there would be precious little left at Larkwood to sell.

No, she could not allow any incipient affection for William to distract her from the more important matters at hand—no matter how appealing he might be.

She realized with astonishment that she truly did find William appealing. It wasn't simply the fact that he had rescued her from humiliation. It was the fact that his actions showed something that she should have known all along: behind his facade of propriety, beneath his overweening concern for correctness, he was a good man.

She wrapped her arms around herself and continued to stare unseeingly at the stage. She had not seen William's best qualities until she had known him for a long while. Perhaps Mr. Wolton had similarly hidden attributes that she would only discover upon further acquaintance.

With that thought in mind, she turned to face her escort and favored him with what she hoped was a warm, encouraging smile. He did not see her, however. He was still scowling at the crowd in the stalls below. It appeared that this unpleasant episode had affected him more deeply than she had thought.

How deeply? she wondered uneasily as she continued to observe him from the corner of her eye. Deeply enough to cause him to doubt the value of her family's good name? Surely not. But as his scowl deepened, a thin tendril of fear began to wind itself around her heart.

ELEVEN

The silence had lasted for at least ten minutes. Finally, Sarah could bear it no longer. "Mr. Wolton, are you well?"

He turned from his contemplation of the London streets and looked at her with troubled eyes. "Yes, quite."

He did not sound well. She thanked heaven that her mother, seemingly oblivious to the embarrassment the Harrisons had just sustained, had decided to accompany several friends to a rout after the play. The only witnesses to what she suspected would be an unpleasant scene were Mr. Wolton's tiger, sitting on the back of the carriage, and his driver, ahead on the box.

There was nothing for it but to ask the question that had been festering in her mind all evening. "Are you concerned about the scene at the theater this evening?"

"Of course I am," he snapped. "Are you not?"

"Somewhat," she said cagily, wishing she had William's skills in diplomacy. What she said in the next few minutes could be the undoing of her entire family. "But such things are soon forgotten. Last week, it was the Queen herself who was subject to a crowd's taunts. Next week some other unfortunate person will be the subject of scorn and ridicule. These things do not last."

His expression was skeptical. "The whispers surrounding you have already lasted several months. I believe you have been the subject of mocking editorials and caricatures since before we met."

"The Season will soon end, and people will forget," she said, trying to keep the desperation she felt from seeping into her voice.

"I was confident that they would have forgotten already. Remember, I am something of an expert when it comes to shocking the *ton*." He sighed and leaned back against the squabs. "But it has been almost three months since Cambermere cried off, and still the scandal continues. I have never made a secret of the fact that I was interested in an alliance between our families mainly as a way of increasing my own respectability."

"And I appreciate your honesty." What could she say to keep him from crying off? She racked her brain for ideas, but none came to mind. Over the course of the last two months, she had done everything she could think of to gloss over her family's disadvantages and to emphasize their attributes. She had to admit that he had a point. It looked as though the scurrilous talk would never go away.

"But this seems to be the sort of thing that has taken on a life of its own. Twenty years from now, people could still be muttering that I had to make do with marrying Cambermere's fortune-hunting jilt."

His words stung like cold Yorkshire sleet. "It is

not my fault—" she began, but he held up his hand.

"I know it is not your fault. You are not the first member of the *ton* to seek to trade a good name for financial salvation, and this disaster with Cambermere was not of your making. But none of that changes the fact that I need to marry someone with an impeccable reputation if I hope to attain the status that I feel is my right." He frowned. "I have as much or more wealth than many peers and a home that is the envy of most, but without an elevated pedigree, my heirs will be little better than their father—a money-grubbing Cit with pretensions." His voice was so sad that she longed to comfort him.

"Better a Cit with money than an earl's daughter with none."

He responded to her sally with a weak smile. "Truly, Lady Sarah, I wish I could pursue my suit. But the Season will end soon, and I am not exactly the sort of person who attracts many invitations to shoot in Scotland or spend extended stays in country houses. If I do not manage to engage the affections of a suitable lady within the next month, it shall be another year before I have a good opportunity to try again. I am one-and-thirty. I do not have a lifetime to spend in this pursuit."

Even as her brain registered his words, Sarah's thoughts were racing ahead. Everything he said made eminent sense. And she could not fault him, as he had been completely candid about his intentions from the beginning.

But the letter . . . the news of Father selling Daisy . . . there would be no salvation for the Harrisons. She would have to write to her father this very night, tell him of her failure, advise him to start inquiries to learn who might be interested in leasing Larkwood.

Leasing Larkwood. She swallowed.

"I understand your concerns, sir, but I ask you to reconsider," she said to Mr. Wolton with as much dignity as she could muster in the circumstances. It had come to this. She was little better than a beggar, just as the crowd had said.

"I cannot," he said, grasping her hand. "You are a charming young woman, Lady Sarah, and any gentleman would be fortunate to have you as his wife. But a man such as I cannot simply marry any lady who catches his fancy. Marriage is one of the only bargaining chips at my disposal. I cannot simply throw it away."

Throw it away. Her fortunes had fallen so low that even a man with a scandalous reputation considered marrying her to be a waste of effort.

Not only had she failed to find a fortune to save her family. It was also looking increasingly unlikely that she would marry anyone. She would be an impoverished ape-leader to the end of her days.

She squared her shoulders. That future would not come to pass if she could help it. Her family had been in dire straits for years, and she had not given up hope in all that time. She would not do so now. England was a large country. Surely there was some rich gentleman, somewhere in the provinces, who did not read the papers and could be swayed by some gentle persuasion.

"Thank you for your honesty, Mr. Wolton, and for your kind words," she said in a quiet voice. "I wish you the best of luck on your quest, and all happiness in the future."

"As I wish you," he said, squeezing her hand and releasing his breath. He was clearly relieved that the worst was over.

As was she, in a curious way. For months now, she had hoped and dreamed and prayed that Mr. Wolton would offer for her. But now that it was clear that he never would, a small, hidden part of her was glad. It was wicked to care so much about her personal happiness when her family's future was in the balance. But she could not deny that she felt a lightness and a freedom in the knowledge that she would not be required to spend her days looking the other way as Mr. Wolton continued his relationship with his mistress and spent his days in White's, wagering untold sums on cards. And that she would not have to spend nights engaged in what her mother had described obliquely as her "wifely duties." Sarah had little idea what those might entail, but she knew they would involve the sorts of amorous embraces she had observed along the towpath in Richmond. And that thought had not been enticing.

Not the way thoughts of embracing William in a similar manner have intrigued you, a traitorous voice in her head murmured.

She ignored the voice, as she had for many weeks, and gave Mr. Wolton what she hoped was an encouraging smile. The very last straw would be to face his pity, on top of everything else. She took a deep breath and concentrated on presenting a strong, confident facade as she willed the carriage to make quick progress back to Chelsea.

* * *

Later that evening, alone in her room at Mrs. Templeton's home, Sarah's composure cracked. Fortunately, she had managed to complete the journey home before dissolving into what became a torrent of tears. And, doubly fortunately, no one save Mrs. Templeton's lady's maid had been witness to her distress.

Still, she felt ridiculous. As she had told herself often enough, crying solved nothing. It had felt good, however.

Now that she had released some of her frustration, she felt better able to concentrate on the problem at hand. Unfortunately, she had not devised any practical solutions to her dilemma. She had spent almost two months currying favor with Mr. Wolton. Where was she to find another money-eyed gentleman who would be willing to consider an alliance with her? Her only attribute—her family's sterling reputation—lay in tatters at her feet after tonight's events at the theater. And it would only be further shredded once news of her father's increasing desperation reached London, as it surely would. If she had learned nothing else during her time in Town, she had learned that secrets were very hard to keep among the *ton*.

She had dismissed the maid, telling her that she would prepare for bed on her own. So she stripped off the once-beloved watered-silk dress, which she would never again be able to look at without remembering her humiliation this night. She laid the dress across a chair, picked up her night rail, and put it on. Climbing into bed, she reached for the candle and blew it out.

But sleep was elusive. She would drift toward it, only to hear the taunts of the crowd echoing in her head. "Those who sit with lady beggars . . . lady beggars . . . lady beggars . . ." That, of all the insults, had hurt the most. Because it was true.

Sarah rolled over and pounded her pillow. She had not chosen to become a beggar. It was not she who had spent all the family money on old-fashioned gowns and ridiculous follies. But as soon as that thought crossed her mind, she shook her head.

"I'm sorry," she murmured, even though her parents were not there to hear. It was not she who had lost three children in quick succession. Who had had to deal with crop failure and bad investments. She had no right to criticize her parents for the ways they had coped with their tragedies.

All she could do was help extricate them from financial ruin. But how?

"Lady beggars . . . lady beggars . . . lady beggars."

That was it.

All of London already thought her little better than a street urchin. What harm could it do to apply to Lord Cambermere for the funds that were rightfully hers? Now that he had destroyed her hopes of a good marriage by returning to Town, the least he could do was provide for her as he had promised.

True, she had no proof of his promise. But she had to hope that, somewhere, he had a shred of his brother's honor and decency. That somehow, he would take responsibility for the disaster he had created.

She swallowed. Going to beg money from the man who had jilted her was going to be one of the hardest things she had ever done. But she knew she would not be able to live with herself if her family lost their house because she was too proud to avail herself of the last option open to her. She would call on the duke tomorrow, she resolved.

As a hazy London dawn filtered through the curtains, Sarah finally drifted into a dreamless sleep.

Sarah watched as the hired hack drove away and left her standing on the pavement in front of Cambermere House.

Mrs. Templeton would have been happy to let her use the family carriage for her expedition, but Sarah didn't want anyone to know where she was going or why. If she succeeded, she would share the good news. If she failed, it would be completely mortifying.

Foolish girl, she said to herself as she approached the huge mansion that dominated one of Mayfair's prettiest squares. *You should be used to mortification by now.*

She climbed the few steps and rapped on the shiny red door with an equally shiny brass knocker. Instantly, the door swung open, and a sandy-haired butler stood before her. "Yes?"

Sarah swallowed. She had come this far. It was too late to turn back. "I am here to see His Grace."

The butler eyed her. "And is he expecting you?"

I doubt it. She shook her head.

"How shall I announce you?" The butler's voice was still perfectly correct, but what little warmth had been in it had evaporated.

"Please tell him Lady Sarah Harrison is here."

That got a reaction. "Oh, yes, of course, of course, Lady Sarah," he said in a rush. He opened the door wide, ushered her in, and closed it quickly behind her. "My apologies for my cool welcome."

At least the duke's servants had the good manners to be embarrassed in her presence, even if their employer did not.

"His Grace often gets callers whom I must turn away," the butler continued, his face a dull red. "Petitioners of all sorts—you can just imagine."

Indeed she could. "Do not give it a moment's thought."

"Please, come into the yellow salon and be seated. Would you like some tea?"

A hot beverage might be all she would be able to wrest from Lord Cambermere. "Yes, thank you."

Within moments, she was seated in a bright, airy room just off the main foyer. She took in the butter yellow walls, the elaborate plasterwork ceiling, and the pristine furniture upholstered in charming garnet and cream stripes. Underfoot, a soft cream carpet looked as though it had never seen a human footstep, much less a speck of dirt.

What would it have been like to be mistress of such a home? Not as much fun as it might seem, if one had to accept the Duke of Cambermere as part of the package, Sarah decided.

The door to the room opened to admit a gray-haired woman garbed in sober black, carrying a laden tray. A ring of keys dangled from her substantial waist. It appeared that the housekeeper herself had taken on the task of bringing Sarah's tea.

"Good afternoon, Lady Sarah," she said, setting the tray on a low Sheraton table and bobbing a curtsey. "Welcome to Cambermere House." As she rose, she surveyed Sarah quickly from head to toe. A full report to the rest of the servants below stairs would no doubt be forthcoming.

"Thank you." Sarah smiled warmly at the older woman. It could not be easy, working in the home of the Wild Duke. She suspected that the staff needed all the human kindness they could get.

"Is the tray to your liking, m'lady? There's ginger biscuits and lemon cake here, and I could fetch some poppyseed cakes, if you like."

Sarah shook her head. "This is lovely, thank you."

The servant hesitated for a moment. Then, apparently unable to think of another reason to linger, she curtsied again and quit the room.

I likely won't have time to sample more than a ginger-snap before I am evicted from the house, Sarah thought as she poured tea from an elegant blue teapot into a china mug so fine she could see through it.

On that point, she was wrong. She waited a full fifteen minutes—she noted the time on the ornate ormolu clock on the mantelpiece—before the door opened again. She took a deep breath and wiped her damp hands along her skirts as she girded herself to meet her former fiancé.

But the person who came through the door was not Lord Cambermere, but his wife. When the duchess closed the door behind her, Sarah realized that the duke was not even going to deign to see her. Her thudding heart plummeted to the toes of her half boots. The fact that he had sent an emissary to face her did not bode well for her success.

That thought was quickly replaced by another. He had jilted her, scorned her, and made her the laughingstock of London, and yet he didn't even have the backbone to look her in the eye. What kind of a man *was* he? First he sent William to Yorkshire. Now he sent his own wife to solve his problems.

A man with so little honor *deserved* to be shamed into living up to his commitments. It was about time that George Cates, Duke of Cambermere, learned to take responsibility for his actions.

Lady Cambermere leaned against the door for a moment before proceeding into the room. "Lady Sarah," she said. "I wish we were meeting under more favorable circumstances." She crossed the room and took a seat on the edge of a large settee.

"I must apologize for that terrible scene at the theater last night," she continued, her voice cool and not sounding terribly penitent. "I am used to dealing with hostile audiences, but I am certain that you are not. If I had known that you would be there, and that the crowd would turn on you, I would not have attended the performance."

Sarah waved away her words. She had to get right to the point of her visit, before she lost her nerve. "Thank you, your grace, but I am not here for apologies. I am here to demand financial restitution."

The duchess's blue eyes turned cold, and her voice when next she spoke was frosty. "By law, my husband owes you nothing."

Sarah was prepared for this argument. She had practiced her riposte in the hack on the way to Cambermere House. "That is true, but an honorable gentleman's word is his bond. Lord Cambermere verbally promised my father a handsome settlement, and whether a piece of paper attests to that fact or not makes no difference to me." Sarah swallowed. Every word felt like a nail lodged in her throat.

Lady beggar, lady beggar, lady beggar.

She was *not* begging. She was simply demanding what was rightfully hers.

"As I understand it, William allowed you to keep the Cambermere betrothal ring. That should have been *mine*, but I have not complained." The duchess helped herself to a gingersnap and settled back into her seat.

Sarah decided not to point out that the law was completely on her side in the matter of the ring. She had bigger fish to fry, and it appeared that stronger means would be necessary to extract the settlement she had been promised.

"Lady Cambermere, there has been some, er, talk about the, um, hastiness of your marriage. It could do your reputation no good to have it become known about Town that your husband does not live up to his promises."

The duchess leaned forward, a cold glint in her pale blue eyes. "If you mean that scene at the theater last night, or the mutterings of a few disgruntled newspaper writers, I am impervious, as is my husband. We have both withstood scandal before, and likely will again. When all is said and done, we are still the Duke and Duchess of Cambermere, and there will always be people who will make us welcome."

No one says no to a duke . . . or a duchess, Sarah thought. "But my family—" she began, loathing the desperate undertone in her voice.

"—is none of my concern," the duchess said. "Really, Lady Sarah, if your parents had been more prudent with their money, they wouldn't need to send their daughter crawling to every rich man in London to trade her virtue for a fat purse."

Sarah set her teacup on the table with a clatter and stood so swiftly that Lady Cambermere shrank back in her seat. "You would be wise not to speak carelessly of things you don't understand," she said through gritted teeth. For the first time in her life, she wished she had an unbuttoned fleuret at her side. "I have not traded my virtue for anything, and you do not know the first thing about my parents."

Lady Cambermere stood as well, her face so close to Sarah's that it was possible to see the stains on her teeth. For the first time, Sarah caught a very faint odor of wine. "I have worked too hard, for too many years, to marry Lord Cambermere. If you think I am going to relinquish one farthing to a money-grubbing provincial chit like you, *you* do not know the first thing about *me.*"

The duchess glared at Sarah for a moment longer, but when Sarah didn't flinch, she moved toward the mantelpiece and leaned against it.

"If you think the scandal now is humiliating, you would be wise to leave London and never bother my husband again. I know the ways of newspapermen far better than you do. And at least a few of them owe me for . . . favors," she said with a smug smile. "A few choice rumors planted in a few avid ears, and your family would lose more than their house."

Despite her best efforts, Sarah felt faint. It had been a dreadful mistake to come here. What had she done?

"That will not be necessary," she heard herself say. "Nothing would induce me ever to cross the threshold of Cambermere House again." As she said it, she realized it was true. Nothing was worth dealing with such odious people as the duke and duchess—not even saving Larkwood. She would just have to find another solution.

She moved toward the door, having had the last word. If nothing else, she would leave of her own volition, before the duchess had a chance to throw her out. Without another word, she yanked the door open and stalked out.

Fortunately, she had brought neither coat nor parasol, so she did not need to wait for the butler to provide them. She strode across the echoing foyer and headed for the door, praying that she would make it out of the house before anyone saw the hot tears streaking down her cheeks.

After what seemed like a year, she reached the front door, opened it, and stepped into the warm summer sunshine—and straight into Lord William's broad chest.

TWELVE

A coarse word Sarah had never even *thought* before flitted through her brain.

"Sarah!" William caught her by both elbows as the door to Cambermere House swung shut behind her. "Are you all right?"

She nodded. "I've a cold. It makes my eyes runny."

He gave this feeble excuse the raised eyebrows it deserved. "What on earth are you doing here?"

She shook her head. She could not let William see what an abject creature she had become. The last remaining shred of her pride made her say, "I just came to pay my respects to the new duchess."

"My nurse used to tell me better fairy tales." His voice was soft and encouraging.

"Well, this one will have to suffice for today." She took a deep, shuddering breath, and tried to ignore the faint scent of sandalwood that filled her consciousness and brought so many memories rushing back. Another deep breath steadied her enough that she could look directly into William's face. "Thank you, William, for your actions last night at the theater. Your handling of the crowd was masterful, and I owe you a very deep debt of gratitude."

He smiled. "As the Cates family was the initial cause of the disturbance, I believe we owe you an apology." He looked more closely at her face, and lifted his thumb to wipe away a tear she could feel trembling on the edge of her chin. "I suspect, however, that no such contrition will be coming from my brother or his wife, so unfortunately, my deep regret will have to do."

"Thank you, truly." How could one brother be such a scoundrel and the other so honorable?

"Believe me, I meant to warn you that George was home," William continued. "He and Harriet arrived late yesterday afternoon and insisted on going to the theater that very night. Harriet could not be dissuaded from seeing this new actor everyone is talking about. If I had had any idea that you would be there, too, I would have found some way to talk them out of the idea. I should have thought ahead."

"It is no matter." His thumb felt like a red-hot poker against her skin. She had to run, had to hide, had to get away before she dissolved completely under his compassionate gaze. "It is fortuitous that we have met today," she said in a rush. "I will be leaving London in the next few days, and I did want to see you to thank you for all you have done for me in my time here."

"Leaving?" An odd grimace crossed his face. "So am I to wish you happy?"

For a moment, she didn't comprehend his meaning. Happy, on one of the most distressing days of her life? "Oh," she said finally. "No, Mr. Wolton has decided we should not suit. As have Lord Goreham and Lord Finworth."

A spark of something like elation showed in his eyes before he frowned. "But that means you are no closer to solving your family's financial crisis. Do you not wish to stay in London until the end of the Season, to see if perhaps another gentleman—"

She shook her head. "No. That plan has not succeeded, and I doubt that it will no matter how long I stay in London." She looked him squarely in the eye. "I am too scandalous even for the likes of Henry Wolton. I have as much hope of marrying a fortune here as I do of defeating the reigning champion at Angelo's. Less, probably. Every day I stay is a day that I could be spending back at Larkwood, trying to resolve our problems some other way."

The likelihood of finding some other solution was very small, she knew. As the realization hit her anew, a bubble of nausea rose in her throat. All this time in London. All the money she'd spent on this quest. All for naught.

She shuddered and felt a fresh wave of sobs rising. She couldn't let William see her bawling like an infant. She could *not*.

She wrenched herself away from his hand, which still held her right elbow. "And I have so many preparations to make before we depart that I really must return home," she babbled. "I am so glad we saw each other. And I hope that your work in Vienna goes well."

He seized both her arms again. Squeezed. There was nothing for it but to look again into his face. The face she would likely never see again.

She held her breath in an effort to keep from falling apart.

"I am glad we saw each other, too. I was planning to call on you this afternoon. You see, I, too, am leaving London. The day after tomorrow, as a matter of fact."

She exhaled in a rush. "That soon?"

He nodded. "Some complications have arisen regarding accommodations for the English delegation. More and more people are being assigned to attend the talks, and available houses in Vienna are becoming scarce. They want me to precede the main group, to hunt for properties to let, as well as to engage in some further preliminary negotiations with the other parties. Weather permitting, my ship will sail at dawn on Saturday."

As the import of his words sank in, she could do nothing but stare at him. This truly was good-bye. It would be months before he returned to London, and years—if ever—before she did.

She swallowed. "*Bon voyage*, William. And the best of all things—always."

His smile was wistful. "See, you have learned a little French during your stay here. If we'd had more time, perhaps I could have taught you some German as well."

Her eyes were so full of tears that one blink would have them cascading down her face. "You have taught me so much. I can never repay you, nor thank you enough."

"I just wish I could have helped you more." He looked down into her face, and she wondered for one heart-stopping second whether he intended to kiss her again. If he did, she would be lost.

But he didn't. He released his hold on her, picked up her hand, and brushed his lips across her gloved knuckles. When he looked up again, his face was distraught.

"Goodbye, Sarah. I, too, wish the best of all things for you. And if you ever need help, in any capacity, do not hesitate to contact me in St. James's. You have my card. My mail will be sent ahead to wherever I am posted."

"Thank you." She did not trust her voice above a whisper.

They faced each other on the doorstep. There was nothing, and everything, left to say.

"I shouldn't delay you any further," she said, moving away from him and backing down the stairs.

"How did you get here? I don't see Mr. Templeton's carriage. And do you not have a maid with you?" His voice was laced with concern.

"I came in a hack." She backed further down the walkway, toward the street. "No one knows that I am gone."

"You can't head back alone," he said, making to follow her.

"No, William, please!" she cried, much more loudly than she had intended. "I will be fine. Please. You don't have to watch out for me anymore." She pivoted and sped down the walk and through the gate, praying he would not follow her.

Tears blinding her, she ran as fast as she could away from Cambermere House. Within several streets of the grand mansion, she heard someone calling her name, but the voice was not William's. Turning around, she saw a small boy in the Cambermere livery. It was the tiger who had accompanied them to Richmond.

"Lord William sez I'm to come with you to Chelsea." The child proudly held up a shiny coin. "He even gave me the fare to go there and back. Said it weren't right for you to walk around London alone."

Another huge sob threatened to engulf Sarah, and this time she did not fight it. Extracting a handkerchief from her reticule, she pressed the square of cool, scented linen to her face as she and the tiger walked more slowly toward Oxford Street.

"George!" William bellowed as he strode across the foyer of Cambermere House. Quinn, the butler, chased after him in a vain effort to retrieve his hat and coat. "George, you scoundrel! Get down here!"

"Lord William, please. There is no need to shout. I will fetch your brother." Quinn glanced about the hall, as if afraid that he would be immediately sacked for this breach of ducal propriety.

William wondered why the butler was so worried. Certainly, in the servant's years at Cambermere House, he had seen much more serious lapses in etiquette than this.

"He shouts for me often enough, when he visits my lodgings. I'm just returning the favor." William strode to the foot of the curving staircase and leaped up the steps two at a time. "George!"

Whatever his brother had done to put Sarah into such a state, William was going to make sure that George took responsibility for his actions, for once in his life. No one had the right to reduce Sarah Harrison to tears.

"Is this noise necessary?" His brother emerged from the drawing room and ambled across the spacious landing. He wore neither neckcloth nor coat, and his shirt was only haphazardly buttoned. "I have a headache that could kill a horse. Come in and be quiet, for God's sake."

"You'll have more than a headache before I'm done with you," William muttered as he followed George back into the drawing room.

"What are you so grim-faced about? I already said I was sorry about the scene at the theater last night. How could I have known the chit would be there? I thought she couldn't *afford* to go to the bloody theater." George tossed himself into a velvet-upholstered chair and settled his feet on a matching ottoman. A glass of something foul-smelling—probably that headache remedy he favored—sat on a nearby table.

"I don't care about last night. What did you say to Lady Sarah this morning?" William sat on a blue settee and fixed his brother with a pointed stare.

George shook his head. "Nothing. Haven't set eyes on the woman."

"I just ran into her at the front door, looking as though she'd been slapped."

"That Harrison woman?" Harriet asked, coming into the room. "If I'd had any idea she was going to be such trouble, I would have sent her away. I thought all she wanted was an apology."

William shifted his gaze from George to Harriet. "*You* spoke to her?"

His sister-in-law shrugged. "George was in no

shape to see anyone. He asked me to find out what she wanted."

William struggled to keep his voice neutral. "And what did she want?"

Harriet laughed, a short, bitter sound devoid of humor. "Money."

For a moment, William couldn't speak. Sarah had swallowed her pride enough to ask George for money? If he'd known she would actually accept anything from Cambermere, he'd have started haranguing George for the money the moment he'd clapped eyes on him yesterday afternoon. But he had just assumed she would throw the money back in their faces.

"I assume you agreed to provide the funds that she was supposed to receive in the marriage settlement," he said, even as he knew how remote that possibility was.

"There was no marriage, and so there was no settlement," Harriet spat. "If we ran around giving money to every woman in England who hoped to marry George, we would be bankrupt within the month. He was quite the prize in the marriage mart," she said, with a look at the duke that turned William's stomach.

He turned his attention to his brother, who appeared unfazed by the news of Harriet's meeting with Sarah. "You will, of course, rectify Harriet's mistake," he said in a cold, hard voice.

"It wasn't a mistake. I told you before. My solicitor burned the papers. She has no proof. And I have responsibilities now. A wife. Harriet needs money for dresses and things. She likes to spend."

I can just imagine, William thought.

"Besides, a friend of mine approached me last night at the interval. Had a great scheme he wanted to talk to me about. Needs some investment in a canal he's building in Wales. Much better use of my funds, if you ask me."

William shot to his feet, almost blind with anger. "Do you realize that the Harrisons will be turned out of their house if they cannot find the money to pay their creditors? Does saving them from ruin not seem like a wise use of your funds? Remember, George, I know your income. You would barely miss the money you promised Sarah. I've seen you lose almost that much in a night of faro."

George opened his bloodshot eyes a bit wider. "*Sarah*, is it? Not *Lady* Sarah? A bit familiar with my ex-fiancée, aren't you, Wills? Maybe hoping to snare a bit of this blunt for yourself by and by? Get the money for her and then marry her, is that your plan? Thought you had more subtlety than that, being a diplomat and all."

In two steps, William had crossed the room and yanked his brother to his feet by the frayed placket of his shirt. "Don't you *dare* say one word against Sarah. You're just very lucky she hasn't sued you in court. Perhaps I should front her the money for that. I have enough to pay a barrister for a nice long public court case."

At that, George blanched. "You wouldn't dare. The scandal would be a big black mark on the Cambermere name. And I know how much stock you put in preserving the family's reputation."

"There's not much left to preserve. Your antics over the last decade had carved away most of it, and marrying your bit of muslin pretty much set the torch to what remained."

"Now see here, Wills," George blustered. "You can't talk about Harriet that way."

"Why not? It's the truth."

"I—" Harriet began.

William released his hold on George's shirt and turned on her. "Don't say one word. Not one."

Realizing when silence was truly golden, Harriet clamped her lips shut.

William turned his attention back to his brother. "Now I'm going to ask you one last time, George. Are you going to send Lady Sarah a bank draft for the full amount of the original settlement?"

"No." George crossed his arms on his chest, looking for all the world like a mulish child refusing to eat his dinner.

"Then I wash my hands of you. This is the last time I shall ever speak to either of you. You need not bother me the next time you land in some unspeakable mess."

If George had looked worried before, he looked panicked now. His hand trembled as he reached for the glass of headache remedy. He downed it in one swallow and set it back on the table with a clatter.

"Now you're really bluffing," he said in a falsely hearty voice. "I hold the purse strings, and I would cut off your income without a second thought."

"I do have investments, and I also earn a modest living through my work in the foreign office." William looked his brother squarely in the eye. "Go ahead."

At his words, an uneasy silence settled on the

room. After a moment, Harriet broke it. "What do you care if he never speaks to you again? Don't let him browbeat you, George."

When George didn't answer, William responded. "He's never bailed himself out of a problem in his life. Our father did it for years, and then I took over the job."

"That's not true!" George blustered.

"Then let me walk away." William's voice was cold. Years of work in the foreign office had given him the sangfroid to deal with situations more perilous than this one. "To tell you the truth, George, I would be relieved."

That was not entirely true. George was a scoundrel without a shred of honor, but he *was* William's closest living relative. And when he was behaving himself, the duke could be quite congenial company.

But if it would help Sarah, William would turn his back on his brother without a second thought.

Silence settled on the trio once again. The faint sounds of traffic in the street below drifted through an open window at the end of the drawing room. William let the quiet lengthen, having learned long ago that humans feel compelled to fill any silence, eventually. He would force his brother to speak first.

A carriage creaked by in the street below.

George tapped his fingertips against the table by his side.

Harriet sighed.

"Fine!" George finally roared. "I'll give the chit what I originally agreed to. But I will have my solicitors draw up papers forbidding her to apply to me for one extra penny. Ever."

"George!" Harriet cried.

"Be quiet!" he snapped. "Do you think I'm happy about this?" He turned his attention to William. "You realize that you are now most deeply in my debt, don't you, Wills?"

William did, and he would think about that later, but for now he could not contain his delight. "Yes, but we'll discuss that another time," he said, grinning. "I have one more request."

"You have a lot of demands," George muttered.

"This one is small." He paused. "Do not mention my role in all this to Lady Sarah." He could at least let her think that George's turnabout had been due to her own efforts. It cost him nothing to salvage that small bit of her pride.

"Since I plan never to communicate with the chit again, that poses no problem." George sank back farther in his chair.

"Good. Now you'd better get dressed," William said.

"Dressed? What for? I feel like the very devil."

"If you want to go to the bank en dishabille, that's your business. But you might cut a better figure if you at least put on a coat."

THIRTEEN

Sarah sat at the small writing desk in a corner of Mrs. Templeton's front parlor, finishing her daily letter to Hester. She had tried to keep her message cheerful; it would do no good to worry her sister unduly. But she had rarely had less occasion to feel optimistic.

Her interview with Lady Cambermere the previous day still made her feel ill whenever she thought about it. To have come into the house hat in hand, and to have been sent away like a criminal? She had reviewed every aspect of the meeting so often in her mind that she could remember every word. Was there something she could have done differently? Should she have been more deferential?

She stared out the window at the late afternoon bustle of carriages, riders, and pedestrians making their way along Paradise Row. It was no good trying to undo what was done, she told herself for the tenth time in as many minutes.

She wished they were returning to Yorkshire today. However, her mother wanted to attend a dinner hosted by a childhood friend later in the week, and Sarah hadn't had the heart to insist on an early departure. Her mother had asked for so little during their stay in London.

What difference would it really make? she asked herself bleakly. Earlier this morning, she had written to her father to advise him to start the preparations to lease Larkwood. By the time she and Lady Glenmont arrived in Yorkshire, the house would already be advertised.

She signed her name to the bottom of the letter to Hester and reached for the small jar of sand at the corner of the desk. Before she could lift it, however, the downstairs maid entered the room and handed Sarah a large cream-colored letter.

"This just arrived for you, Lady Sarah," she said, bobbing a curtsey. "Came by special messenger. He didn't wait for a reply, though."

"Thank you, Betty," Sarah said, accepting the letter. Instantly, she noticed the Cambermere seal in bright red wax.

Her heart sank to her feet. Was this some sort of new threat? What else could the duke and his wife do to her?

The maid nodded and left Sarah alone.

Taking a deep breath, Sarah picked up a silver letter opener, slit the seal, and unfolded the sheet. A second, smaller sheet tumbled out onto the pale green carpet. Sarah ignored it as she focused on the short message scrawled across the thick vellum she held.

Lady Sarah Harrison 17 Paradise Row, Chelsea

Dear Lady Sarah, Enclosed herewith are the funds you requested. Although I feel you have no claim

*upon me, I am forwarding this bank draft as a
goodwill gesture. However, if you attempt to communicate with me further in the future, I shall
take legal action. Yrs, Cambermere*

Funds? Sarah looked down at the piece of paper
that had fluttered to the floor and reached for it
with a shaking hand.

Finally, Lord Cambermere had lived up to his
word. The sum printed on the draft matched the
amount she had been promised when they became
betrothed, to the penny.

For a moment, she could do nothing but stare at
the piece of paper. An irrational corner of her expected it to vanish like a puff of fog if she took her
eyes from it for one second.

Then the full import of the draft dawned on her.
There would be no need to lease Larkwood. No
need for Chadwick to leave Oxford. No need for
her to find a rich husband.

She was *free.* They were all free.

She stood up from her chair so quickly that she
almost tripped over her skirts. Hastening to the
doorway, she hurried through it and down the corridor. On a small table near the front door, her
letter to her father still rested in a lacquered tray.

As giddy as a small child at a Christmas feast, she
grabbed the missive and held it to her chest. There
was no need to send it now.

At that moment, Mrs. Templeton came down the
corridor from the back of the house. "There you
are, Sarah. I wanted to ask whether you could stay
until next week. There's a musicale—"

Before she could finish her thought, Sarah burst

out, "Mrs. Templeton! We can stay forever, if you like! I have just had a letter from Lord Cambermere, with the most astonishing news!" Motioning for her cousin to return with her to the sitting room, she practically ran back down the corridor.

Once again in the room, she picked up the letter and its enclosure and showed them to Mrs. Templeton. The older woman's eyes widened as she scanned the sheet of vellum, then glanced at the bank draft.

"He certainly wasn't gracious about it, was he?" she remarked.

"I could not care if he spat in my face!" Sarah said, barely repressing an urge to spin about the room in glee. "He lived up to his commitment, and that is all that matters." True, she had had to abase herself to bring him to this point, but that was of no import.

Her smile faded. *Was* it her visit yesterday that had brought the duke to this point? Lady Cambermere had certainly seemed unequivocal that there would be no funds forthcoming. And William had told her early in their acquaintance that George was remarkably stubborn and seemed to have made up his mind not to live up to the spirit of the marriage settlement.

So what had changed his mind?

It must have been William.

Sarah dropped into the desk chair with a thump. William had come to her aid, yet again. That was the only explanation. He had deduced the reason for her agitation yesterday, confronted his sister-in-law, and forced the Cambermeres' hand—heaven only knew how.

That meant that he knew that she had come to Cambermere House to beg. A wave of shame, hot and overpowering, swept over her. Even though she knew the duke would eventually tell his brother of her visit, she had hoped that William would hear about it after she left London.

As swiftly as the humiliation overcame her, she dismissed it. What difference did it make if William thought less of her? She had achieved what she had hoped to accomplish by coming to London—she had saved her family from disgrace.

With William's help. She owed him the greatest debt of gratitude, and she had to see him before he left England to give him her thanks in person.

"Mrs. Templeton, would you mind if I sent Fisher to St. James's with a message for Lord William?" Fisher was the Templetons' groom. Normally, such a task would be entrusted to a lesser servant, but Sarah could take no chance that this message would go astray.

"Certainly," Mrs. Templeton said with a knowing look. "You think he played a role in this turn-about?"

Sarah nodded. "I am certain of it."

"I would not be surprised. For you, I suspect Lord William would do even more than this." She paused, as if she was about to say more and then thought better of it. Instead, she headed for the door. "I shall send word to the stable to have Fisher prepare for a quick ride."

Sarah reseated herself at the desk and opened her writing case. Sifting through the jumble of papers within, she finally located William's card. She had never had occasion to write to him before.

She pulled a fresh sheet of stationery toward her. Feeling profligate, she used an entire sheet for her brief message.

Lord William Cates 28 St. James's Street

Dear Lord William, I have a matter of some urgency to discuss with you. If you can spare a few moments before your departure tomorrow morning, I would be delighted if you could visit me in Paradise Row. I shall be at home for the remainder of the day and evening, and look forward to seeing you. Yrs, Sarah Harrison

There. That sounded suitably polite and formal. Quickly, she sanded the letter, blew the grains away, and sealed the missive, just as her cousin returned.

"Fisher will be in the street shortly to deliver your letter," she said. "Shall I have the housekeeper set an extra place for dinner?"

"Perhaps," Sarah said. Lord William's farewell yesterday had seemed final. There was every chance he would not want to see her again.

But he had to. He *had* to. She could not let him leave England before thanking him properly for all that he had done.

With a light heart and high hopes, she headed to the street to give the letter to Fisher.

Six hours later, her hopes had been well and truly dashed.

The little house in Paradise Row was quiet. Mr. Templeton was at a boxing match, and Mrs. Templeton and Lady Glenmont had gone to a friend's house for an evening of cards. They had tried to prevail upon Sarah to join them, but she had waved them on their way with a smile.

"I told Lord William I would be at home," she reminded them.

But it was almost ten in the evening, and she had received no word from William. Perhaps the message had been lost after all.

That had to be the answer. After all, had he not said that she could call upon him anytime? Surely, if he had seen her note, he would have come if he had been at all able. And he would have sent word if he was not.

Her mind whirling in agitation, Sarah paced the sitting room. Could he be angry with her? What had transpired between him and his brother? Had her request caused some sort of irreparable rift?

She could not let William leave London at odds with his brother, due to some fault of hers. She *had* to see him.

But how? She could hardly call upon him at his rooms in St. James's. The neighborhood was not considered suitable for well-bred women even during daylight hours, let alone at night.

Not suitable for well-bred women, she thought. But eminently suitable for well-bred gentlemen.

She dashed out of the sitting room and up the stairs to her small bedroom. Under the window, her trunk stood open. That morning, the upstairs maid had been helping her pack some seldom-used garments in preparation for the return journey to Yorkshire.

Seizing a small lamp from the mantelpiece, Sarah

moved it to the windowsill so that the dim light shone into the trunk. Burrowing under one of her outmoded day dresses and a packet of letters, she groped toward the bottom of the trunk until her hands found the two garments she sought. It had been foolish to bring them all the way to London, but in a rare moment of sentimentality, she had packed them as small mementos of Larkwood.

She had never dreamed she'd have cause to wear them.

William suppressed a huge yawn as he stumbled up the stairs and along the corridor of the building where he leased his rooms. Coming toward him were a pair of young bucks dressed in the height of fashion. Their shirt points were so high William wondered that they didn't injure themselves when they turned their heads.

"Hullo, Cates," one called out as they approached. "You cannot be turning in so early! The night is just beginning."

"I can indeed. I leave tomorrow morning for Vienna, and I need to finish my preparations." The thought of all the tasks still before him made him weary. Castlereagh had kept him at the foreign office until almost ten discussing last-minute details of his journey. William had been awake very late the night before, supervising Stinson as he packed his trunks and winding up various aspects of his London affairs. It would likely be at least six months before he returned to Town, and he did not want to leave anything out of order.

Of course, he would not have had to stay up so

late the previous evening if he hadn't spent most of yesterday afternoon at the bank, ensuring that George carried through on his promise to arrange the bank draft. And then he had felt compelled to go to Cambermere House this morning to ascertain that his brother had actually sent the document to Sarah.

It was a good thing William had made that visit, as the letter and draft had still been sitting on George's desk. The butler had informed him that both George and Harriet were still abed, so William had taken it upon himself to insert the draft into the letter, seal it, and entrust it to a special messenger. He would be damned if he would let George put off this duty one minute more than was necessary.

All that had taken time, however, which was why he had found himself at Whitehall so late on the night before his departure.

With relief, he opened the door to his rooms. Inside, a small lamp glowed in the foyer. Instantly, Stinson appeared through the door leading to the sitting room.

"Good evening, my lord," he said, reaching for his employer's hat and gloves. "I was concerned when you were delayed so long. I trust everything is still in order for the journey tomorrow?"

"It is, at least as far as Castlereagh is concerned," William said, shrugging out of his coat and handing that to the valet as well. "However, I still have much to do here before I retire for the night." It had been a long day, and he longed for more comfortable clothes and a large glass of port. He walked slowly through the foyer to the sitting room, Stinson close on his heels.

"A number of messages that seemed important arrived for you this afternoon," Stinson said.

"I will deal with them in a few minutes," William said wearily, yanking at his neckcloth as he headed down the short corridor to his bedroom.

Ten minutes later, having dispensed with the neckcloth, loosened the high neck of his shirt, and exchanged his stiff waistcoat for his favorite banyan, he felt much more the thing. A glass of port on the table beside him, he sat in a wing chair by the fire, reviewing the day's correspondence. As Stinson had said, there was rather a lot of it, most of it good wishes for a safe journey from his small but loyal circle of friends.

Toward the bottom of the pile he came across a single sheet folded over, sealed in blue wax with the monogram *SH*.

Sarah?

He slit the paper open and read the short message inside. He looked up at Stinson. "When did this arrive?"

Stinson looked at the note. "This afternoon, my lord. 'Twas a grown man who brought it, not a boy. He said Lady Sarah had been very insistent that it reach you today."

Something urgent? Was she in trouble?

He stood. "I will need to go out again after all, Stinson. If you could find me a fresh shirt that has not been packed—"

A sharp rap on the front door interrupted his request. He glanced at the clock on the mantel. Ten forty-five. Who on earth would be calling on him at this hour of the night?

It had to be George. If he wanted to give him a dressing down for sending the letter this morning, William would give back as good as he got. He was far too tired to listen to his brother's excuses tonight. He moved toward the door.

"Let me, my lord," Stinson exclaimed, hurrying after him.

"It's all right," William answered as he strode across the small foyer. "Believe me, it will be my pleasure to deal with George myself, and quickly." He wrenched open the door.

But it was not the duke on the doorstep. The dim lamplight in the hallway revealed a slim youth in a rather ragged shirt and breeches, his face shadowed by an enormous, outdated hat.

"William!" cried the apparition, in a very familiar voice.

"Sarah?" he gasped, immediately scanning the corridor in both directions. None of the other tenants were in view. That was a blessing, at least.

But what in *hell* was he supposed to do with her? He could hardly send her back out into the street. Grabbing her arm, he pulled her into the foyer and slammed the door shut behind her.

"Are you deranged?" he yelled. "Do you have *any* idea what a scandal you could cause if anyone saw you?"

"I was very careful," she mumbled. Her head was bent as she attempted to remove her ridiculous headgear.

"Here, let me help you." He reached for the large tricorn. "Where in the world did you acquire this?"

"It belonged to some long-deceased relative of Mr. Templeton's. One of the maids retrieved it from a storeroom for me." She flinched. "Careful! It's pinned on."

"You mean the Templetons' servants know about this escapade?" he muttered.

The hat bobbed as she nodded. "Of course. I couldn't get here without their help."

"How *did* you get here? Please tell me you didn't take a hack again."

At that, she looked up and fixed him with a withering look. "I do realize how unconventional this trip is. And I may be a country miss, but I do have a modicum of sense. I had Fisher, the Templetons' groom, drive me here. Fortunately, Mr. Templeton rode to his engagement this evening, and Mrs. Templeton and my mother had the coachman drive them in the barouche. The gig was still in the stables."

"You came all the way here in an open gig?" It was all he could do to keep from shaking her. She truly had no idea of how close she had come to ruining herself.

She shrugged. "No one would recognize me in this ensemble. I don't think you did when you opened the door, and you've seen it before."

He scrutinized her a little more closely. "So I have. It's your fencing costume, isn't it?"

She nodded. "There, I think that's the last pin." She removed the hat with a flourish. The haphazard bun she had twisted beneath it tumbled down in its wake. Her hair reached halfway down her back in long chestnut waves.

William stared. In her ugly breeches and threadbare shirt, her hair askew and her face flushed, she was the most beautiful woman he had ever seen. He cleared his throat.

"We can't stand out here in the foyer all night. Come in." As he motioned her into the sitting room, he caught his finger on the neck edge of his banyan. For the first time since he had opened the door, he was suddenly conscious of his state of dishabille.

Really, she had put him in a most embarrassing position. He pulled his banyan closed and cinched the belt more tightly about his waist.

He turned to follow Sarah into the sitting room and caught sight of Stinson lurking near the wardrobe at the back of the foyer. For once, his un-flappable valet appeared struck speechless.

"Tea, Stinson," he muttered. "For Lady Sarah."

"Yes, of course," the goggle-eyed servant replied before heading down the opposite corridor.

"And Stinson?"

He turned. "Yes?"

"Treat this episode as you would one of my diplomatic meetings."

"With the ultimate discretion?"

William nodded.

"Of course, my lord." The servant disappeared into the shadows.

That had been the simple part, William thought as he headed into the sitting room.

Sarah was sitting in a small chair next to the window, looking out onto St. James's Street. With her hair trailing down her back, she looked so innocent and vulnerable.

Vulnerable? Ha! A woman who had the courage

to breach the fortress of St. James's—armored with nothing more than a costume that revealed all too clearly that she was *not* a man—was about as vulnerable as the Duke of Wellington.

"What was Fisher thinking, agreeing to bring you here?" William asked as he lowered himself into the wing chair he had vacated to answer the door.

"He didn't do it gladly," she replied, turning from her contemplation of the scene below. "In fact, it was only when I threatened to walk here on my own that he agreed to accompany me."

"Walk! All the way from Chelsea? If you weren't attacked on the way, you'd have expired of exhaustion."

She laughed. "I had no intention of following through on my threat, but he had no way of divining that. Surely, as a diplomat, you must know that a great portion of negotiation consists in deluding the other party as to your true intentions."

The woman was incorrigible. "That may be true, but he still should not have brought you here. Did he stay?"

"Yes. He's waiting in the street out front."

"At least one thing about this whole affair is rational."

Sarah bristled. "All of it is *rational.* Irregular, I'll grant you, but there is no insanity about it. I had to talk to you, and you didn't answer my letter."

"I returned home not twenty minutes ago and had just read the note and decided to pay you a call when you showed up on my doorstep. Patience is not one of your virtues, is it?"

"I thought perhaps the note had gone missing. I had to see you before you left for Vienna. I did wait for six hours before coming over here. That seems eminently patient to me."

Despite himself, his mouth quirked with amusement. "What was so important that it could not be expressed in a note?" he asked, hoping his voice sounded suitably serious.

She smiled. "I had to thank you in person for the bank draft. That was beyond kind."

"I did not write the draft. It came from George."

Her grin widened. "It may be his signature at the bottom, but for all intents and purposes, it came from you. Lady Cambermere was unequivocal in her refusal of my request. And from what you've told me of the duke's character, I suspect he did not provide this money willingly, either."

He nodded. "I can't deny that."

"So you must have used your skills in persuasion to convince him. I do not know how you did it, but I am most grateful."

"I told George I would never speak to him again if he did not live up to the spirit of your aborted marriage settlement." He picked up the glass of port he had been drinking while reading his correspondence and took a deep draft.

Her eyes were wide in a face made pale by dim candlelight. "You would disown your only brother for me?" she whispered. "But he could have threatened to cut off your income."

"He did. Threaten, that is," he added quickly when he heard her gasp. "Fortunately, we came to an agreement. I will continue to speak to him, and he will continue to forward my allowance. It worked out well for all concerned."

"But why?" She stood and crossed the room toward him. "Why would you risk your family and your livelihood for me?"

That was a question he did not want to explore in any detail, now or ever. "It was truly not much of a risk. Although it might sound self-important, I'm valuable to George. I know people who can help him when he gets into trouble, and I have a cooler head in a crisis than he does. Since it seems likely that he will continue to get in trouble for the rest of his life, he needs to keep me in his corner."

He leaned forward in the chair, realized that that made the banyan gape in a most indiscreet manner, and leaned back again. "As for the income, it makes my life more comfortable, but I could live without it. I have investments and a moderate income from the foreign office. I doubt I would starve on the street."

"All the same—" She knelt down beside him, far closer than was prudent. He remembered how her skin had felt beneath his fingers, that afternoon in the carriage at Richmond.

"I was honored to do it, Sarah." He cleared his throat, sipped his port, and looked away from her. "You deserve to be happy."

She said nothing in response. The silence grew, until the ticking of the small silver clock on the mantel seemed inordinately loud.

Demmed schemer. She was using his own trick of extended silence to spur him into speaking further, or at least into looking at her. Well, it would not work. He was the master of that tactic.

The clock continued to tick. He would not look at her. It would be unwise.

A chime rang out from the mantel, then another,

until eleven had sounded. As the last note evaporated on the warm summer air, he gave into temptation and glanced at her.

She smiled at him, a smile of such gratitude that he was at a loss as to how to respond.

"You've given me and my family our lives back," she murmured. "I will never be able to even begin to repay you for your kindness."

He chuckled. "I was simply preserving my family's reputation. That's all."

Sarah shook her head. "Other people may believe that—George, Harriet, your colleagues at Whitehall. Perhaps even *you* believe it. But I know differently. You don't do these things out of pride alone. You do them because you're an honorable man. A *good* man." Hesitantly, she reached for his hand, which was resting on his knee, and squeezed it.

If she hadn't touched him, he would have been fine. But her small, smooth hand wrapped around his own unnerved him. He found himself wondering what it would be like to kiss her again, one last time.

It would be wonderful. And very, very foolish.

He extricated his hand, picked up his glass, and moved toward the trolley of decanters next to the window, more to put some distance between himself and Sarah than because he really wanted another glass of wine. Nonetheless, he picked up a crystal bottle, took out the stopper, and refilled his glass before speaking.

"Thank you for your kind words," he said, his voice sounding gruff and prudish, even in his own ears. When had he become so stiff-rumped?

She stared at him from her place beside his chair. "They were more than just words," she said. "I meant every one."

"And I mean this, as well," he said, crossing the room again and sitting a safe distance from her, on a small settee. "You are a formidable, fearless woman, Sarah, and it has been my great pleasure to have met you."

She stood. "So this is good-bye."

He nodded, even as every muscle, every sinew, every nerve in his body screamed out for him to go to her. He knew, without a word having been spoken, that if he offered for her again, this time she would say yes. She no longer had her family's finances to worry about, and her eyes were bright with an emotion he had seen some wives train on their husbands, but never expected to see focused on him.

Understandably, she was grateful to him. Unmistakably, they were drawn to each other—that afternoon in Richmond had left him in no doubt of that. She had probably mistaken those feelings for love. It would be so very easy to do.

But a match between them would be a terrible, terrible mistake. She had never wanted to leave Yorkshire. He spent more time living out of trunks than he did by his own fireside.

He—and by extension, any spouse he might take—needed to be the soul of propriety if he was to have any gravitas and credibility as a diplomat. And Sarah would not be Sarah if she had to behave like a milk-and-water miss. As he'd realized long before, she was whiskey and fire. He'd be damned if he'd dilute her.

Even if the look on her face was so very, very tempting.

"I think you should go now," he said in a strangled rush. "I'll go down to the street to alert Fisher that you are on your way." With a brief nod, he walked by her, through the foyer, and out the front door. When he returned to his rooms five minutes later, she was in the foyer, finishing the job of jamming her curls under the tricorn hat.

"Goodbye, William," she said, her eyes shiny. "Be happy."

He swallowed past the lump that had suddenly formed in his throat. "Have a safe journey back to Yorkshire. And good luck."

They stood like two statues in the foyer, afraid to move, afraid to touch, afraid to stay or go.

"You should hurry. Fisher has untied the horse."

She nodded, her gaze never leaving his face.

"I'll escort you to the street."

"That's not necessary." Her voice was taut.

"In that ensemble, you won't be safe if you run into any foxed young bucks," he said. "Not one man in a thousand will mistake you for a man for anything longer than a second." Despite his best efforts, he allowed himself one last, quick look at the pleasing picture she presented in her thin shirt and snug inexpressibles. Then he opened the door and motioned her through it.

They passed through the corridor and down the stairs in silence. When they left the building, Fisher was at the pavement, holding the horse's bridle.

"Ready, Lady Sarah?" he asked.

She looked William squarely in the eyes. When he did not say anything, she answered, "Yes, Fisher."

Then she turned around, accepted the groom's help into the gig, and sat down against the tufted seat.

The groom hopped onto the seat beside her.

"Quickly, Fisher, if you can," William murmured.

"Aye, sir," the groom nodded, with a wary glance at his passenger.

Moments later, the carriage pulled away from the pavement. Sarah looked at William once more, then turned her eyes toward the passing street scene. A moment later, the carriage disappeared into the swarming traffic, and William was alone.

He stared after the gig for a moment or two, then returned to his rooms. There was a lot of packing to do before the ship sailed in the morning, and he had no time to waste standing in the middle of St. James's Street, spinning dreams about what might have been.

FOURTEEN

The late October air was crisp and scented with wood smoke as the carriage rolled through yet another cobblestone square. Even though the day was cool, Sarah had wanted to enjoy the brilliant sunshine and had asked the driver to leave the head of the carriage folded back.

"Tell me the address again, Mrs. Templeton. I want to make sure he takes us to the right house," Sarah said.

Her companion consulted a scrap of paper in her lap. "Twenty-nine Friedrichstrasse."

Sarah laughed. "I shall never figure out how to say 'Twenty-nine' in German. May I have the paper, please?"

Her cousin laughed as well and passed her the scrap. Sarah passed it forward to the young blond driver of their hired carriage, who nodded, smiled, and handed it back.

"Can you believe we're almost there?" she asked her cousin.

"No, I cannot. I must confess, there were times in the last three weeks when I thought that we would never arrive." She smiled. "And if I was impatient, I can only imagine how impatient you were."

Sarah grinned. "All my excitement may well be for naught. This may be a fool's errand."

"Possibly, but I have a suspicion it won't be." Mrs. Templeton opened up her voluminous reticule and began digging in it for something, likely money to pay the driver. Sarah turned her attention back to the passing scene.

Her first impressions of Vienna had been much like those she had experienced when arriving in London, she thought. All that she could comprehend at first were crowds of people, endless streets, clots of carriages. But slowly some differences emerged. There were snow white houses that looked like fanciful cakes, with towers and turrets and swooping decorations. There were grand boulevards lined with trees Sarah couldn't identify. And every street corner seemed to boast a shop selling *kaffee*, which she had quickly deduced was the German word for coffee.

Vienna differed greatly from Rotterdam, or Prague, or any of a number of cities they had passed through on their way from London. It had been a long journey, and Sarah had to admit that the first few days had been as trying as anything she had ever experienced. The ship across the Channel had almost been her undoing.

"Is it always this uncomfortable?" she had gasped to Mrs. Templeton on the first night as the ship heaved and rocked during a tremendous thunderstorm.

Her companion had shaken her head. "Not always. Sailing can be quite pleasant."

Sarah decided to hold onto that thought for future reference and consolation.

Once they had arrived in Rotterdam, however, things improved. Fisher, Mrs. Templeton's groom, had accompanied them on the journey. He took care of arranging for fresh carriages and horses, and for a place to stay each evening. Since none of them spoke any of the languages of the countries through which they passed, they made a game of trying to guess the meaning of words printed on shop signs and street corners. It had passed the time, and Sarah had discovered that she found languages intriguing. Such an interest would serve her well if—

She decided not to think about the *ifs* that had dogged her during the long weeks of their journey. *If* William would agree to see her. *If* he would accept that she had changed. *If* she could live up to his standards—and *if* he could give her the freedom she would always need, to some degree.

This journey might well turn out to be a waste. But she had had no choice but to try.

The driver turned around in his seat and smiled at them. "Not far now," he said in halting English. "Soon."

Soon. Sarah's breath came in short bursts. Would William be impressed with the effort she had made—or see it as just one more example of her impetuousness?

Dusk was falling when William returned to his rented town house. He was home earlier than usual tonight; a meeting with a man who owned a number of properties throughout Vienna had gone better than he had hoped and thus had ended earlier than expected. So he would be able to enjoy a warm dinner at a civilized hour and still have time to clear up a little bit of work before retiring for the night. All in all, it had been a good day, he thought as he opened the door that led into the small stucco town house he had leased near the center of Vienna.

Thoughts of dinner and productive work were cheering, but thoughts of returning to this empty house were not. Strangely, he had never found his rooms in St. James's lonely. Nor had any of the other places he had stayed over the years felt bleak. But this house did.

He had tried for weeks to pinpoint the source of his unease. At various times, he had attributed it to the florid architecture, to the neighborhood, to the eerie quietness of his neighbors. Then he had dismissed these arguments, one by one. The only explanation, he was finally forced to concede, was that he missed Sarah. Her arrival in his life since his last trip overseas had changed everything.

He had thought countless times about that last evening, in his rooms in St. James's Street. If he had but said the word, they might already be married.

And they might already be miserable.

The journey to Vienna had been long and difficult, and the round of social events had been even more staid than usual. Sarah would have tried to put a good face on things, but she would have been exhausted by the journey and bored witless by the diplomats' wives and their idle gossip of Vienna.

It would have been a recipe for disaster. As he did every night, he congratulated himself on his cool assessment of the pros and cons of the situation, and on the eminently rational decision he had made. Unlike George, he had not allowed emotion to cloud his judgment when it came to the matter of picking a wife.

He closed the door behind him. The tiny vestibule was empty. Stinson must be busy at the back of the house, arguing with the cook as he did this time each day. His valet had very specific ideas about what constituted a proper evening meal for an Englishman, and he never tired of trying to make the Hungarian cook they had hired aware of these rules.

William chuckled to himself as he unwound his muffler and hung up his own coat and hat. He really should do more to convince Stinson that he should be at the door to greet his employer at the end of each day, but since William's schedule was so erratic, he held no ill will against the valet. And there were days—such as this one—when he welcomed the opportunity to arrive home in peace. Stinson had an unfortunate propensity to pepper one with questions before one had fully shaken off the cares of the day.

William spotted a copy of the *Morning Post* on the small table in the vestibule and checked the date on the front page. Two weeks ago. It must have just arrived in today's post. Excellent. He would have something to read before his dinner.

Tucking the journal under his arm, he went up the steps to the reception rooms on the second floor, intending to stretch out on the chaise longue in the sitting room to enjoy the newspaper. But as he entered the sitting room, he saw that someone else was already ensconced on that particular piece of furniture.

"Since my attire disturbed you so much the last time I paid you a visit, I thought I'd wear something more conventional this time," said Sarah as she stood and crossed the room to greet him, her very proper green silk skirts rustling.

For one of the few times in his life, he was speechless.

"What on earth are you doing here?" he finally sputtered.

She grinned. "That's a lovely greeting for a friend who has made her way through half a dozen countries just to pay a call." Despite her smile, she seemed uncertain. She stopped a few feet from him and clasped her hands in front of her.

"My curiosity seems natural. I am almost certain you did not mention any plans to travel to Vienna when last we met." He tapped a finger against his head. "No, I am certain I would have remembered that."

A tiny smile played about her lips. "I came to the decision after we spoke last—in the Templetons' gig on the way back to Chelsea, as a matter of fact. It just took me a few months to set the plans in motion. I had to return to Yorkshire first, to put some affairs in order."

He could barely comprehend her words because his mind was racing. "Is anyone here with you?" he asked, glancing around the room. Surely she hadn't made a journey of hundreds of miles without aid or chaperone?

"Not here in this room, at this moment. But yes, I do have company. Mrs. Templeton and Fisher are ensconced in a hotel, several streets from here. Fisher walked me here; he will return to escort me back to the hostelry, if I send him a note."

"Don't send for him just yet." He dropped into a gilt-trimmed chair. "You still haven't answered my first question. Why are you in Vienna?"

She pursed her lips, as though deciding how much—if any—of the truth to reveal. Then she let out her breath with a large whoosh.

"I made the journey in order to show you that I could." Her voice was more hesitant than he had ever heard it.

"Pardon me?" What she had said made no sense.

"You were convinced that I could not adapt to travel, and that that was sufficient reason why we should not suit. I wanted to convince you that I could." She returned to the chaise and sat down. "And, truly, after the first few days I did get used to it. It has been fascinating, actually, hearing all the different languages and trying different foods. Did you know that they eat cheese and hard rolls for breakfast in Germany? I found it most odd."

He ignored her culinary question to focus on the main part of her extraordinary explanation. "You wanted to prove to me that you could travel?"

She nodded. "Yes. You seemed to think that my hatred of travel was a permanent condition. But I believe travel is like broccoli."

He blinked, unable for the third time in as many minutes to follow a turn in the conversation. "How so?" he asked.

"It isn't terribly appealing at first, but the more you taste it, the more you like it."

He laughed, a loud, barking, rusty sound. Lord, he had missed her.

"But like broccoli, one can get too much of a good thing." He sighed. It was so tempting to succumb to her obvious efforts to overcome his good sense. Already, the house seemed brighter and more cheerful, just because she was here. But he couldn't let her do this. She deserved a better life than the one he could offer her.

"I don't just travel occasionally, Sarah," he began. "I travel for a living. My life is one long series of carriage rides over bumpy, unfamiliar roads. I've spent more time on ships than I care to remember. Half the time, I reach for some book or article of clothing only to realize I've left it five hundred miles behind me in another set of rooms, in another city, in another country."

"I know all this. I knew it when I left London three weeks ago." Her face was maddeningly serene.

"But—"

She held up a hand to forestall him. "Please, let me finish."

He nodded. "Go on."

"I know it is hard to believe that I could change my attitude to travel. And truly, I must confess that I enjoy it more than I did previously, but I doubt I shall ever come to love it as you do."

"You see—"

She gave him a mockingly severe look, and he stopped. He had promised to let her have her say.

"But I've changed so much in the last year, William." She leaned forward, her elbows on her knees in a most unladylike manner. "When you first knew me, would I have begged money from George?"

He shook his head.

"Would I have waltzed before a crowd of strangers?"

"No."

"I did those things, and so many more, because you helped me see that I could. I am so much more, now, than the sheltered, provincial miss you met in Yorkshire. I have more courage than I ever had before."

He laughed. "I've seen you fence. Courage is one thing you have never lacked."

"Physical courage is a small matter." She inhaled so deeply he could hear her intake of breath from the other side of the room. "But a year ago, I would have never been brave enough, in my heart, to undertake a journey of a thousand miles to tell a man I loved him, when I have no idea if he even returns my affections."

She stopped speaking. Yearning, hope, and fear were written clearly in her eyes.

He leaned back in his chair as a wave of emotion washed over him with such unaccustomed force that he almost could not breathe.

When they had met last in London, he had resisted the temptation to gather her up in his arms, and he had thought that that was the hardest thing he had ever done. But it was so difficult to resist the urge to embrace her now that he had to grip the arms of his chair to keep from flying out of it.

"Sarah—"

"I know what you are going to say." Her voice was soft, and when he looked at her, his heart twisted when he saw that her eyes were bright with unshed tears.

"You're going to tell me that I'm too wild a woman for your little world of prim diplomats." Her smile was sad. "And perhaps I am. I would do my very best to behave as a proper young wife, but I cannot guarantee that I would not misstep a few times."

She paused, leaned back in the chair and sighed. "But perhaps a few missteps in life aren't all wrong. As long as no one is hurt, perhaps they are the reason we feel alive."

He thought of the "missteps" he had shared with her. The fencing practice in Yorkshire. The embrace in Richmond. That last illicit encounter in St. James's. Could he say, truly, that he regretted any of them?

No, he could not. In fact, they stood out in his mind in vivid relief, in the midst of a monotonous series of gray, indistinguishable days.

Perhaps she was right. As George's brother, he had grown to fear every minute step outside society's boundaries. But George's steps were leaps into disaster. Sarah's were not.

As she'd said long ago, improprieties in private harmed no one. But more than that, they brought a joy and variety to living that he had never realized he missed, until they were gone.

Until she was gone.

She stood. "I am so sorry," she whispered, swallowing. "I should never have come here. After all you have done for me, all I have done is embarrass you." She picked up her skirts in a clear effort to dash for the door.

Swiftly, he moved across the room and blocked her way.

"You haven't embarrassed me," he said as she slammed into his chest. Lord, she felt good. So soft and warm.

He wrapped his arms around her, as he had longed to do every day—and every night—since that afternoon in Richmond.

"If I'm embarrassed, it's only because it took me so long to see that you are the greatest breath of fresh air that ever blew into my stodgy, hidebound life," he murmured against her hair. "I'm embarrassed because you had to make such a long, difficult journey, just to open my eyes."

She pulled away from him. "Well, perhaps I'm glad I embarrassed you, then."

He chuckled, realizing that he laughed more in her company in five minutes than he did in the company of his diplomatic colleagues in a month. As he looked down at her, however, he realized that he had more things on his mind than mirth. He gave in to his very human instincts and kissed her.

It was just as sweet as he remembered.

"Do you truly think you could be happy with a stuffy old stick like me?" he said as they finally parted, some moments later.

She nodded. "Do you truly think I would have come all this way if I didn't think I could be?"

He wrapped his arms around her waist. "Marry me, Sarah. Teach me how to make mistakes."

She laughed and threaded her fingers through his hair. "If that is what you wish to learn, you have picked an excellent teacher."